THE DREAM MISTRESS

The Dream Mistress

JENNY DISKI

Weidenfeld and Nicolson
London

First published in Great Britain in 1996 by
Weidenfeld & Nicolson

The Orion Publishing Group Ltd
Orion House
5 Upper Saint Martin's Lane
London WC2H 9EA

ISBN 0 297 81709 4

A catalogue record for this book
is available from the British Library

Typeset at The Spartan Press Ltd,
Lymington, Hants

Printed in Great Britain
by Clays Ltd, St Ives plc

. . . those dreams best fulfil their function about which one knows nothing after waking.

Sigmund Freud

1

Mimi woke suddenly to find the screen a blank uniform green and the lights on. Something by Mozart – a quartet – was playing. Ahead of her the rows of plush red seats were tipped up and the aisles to either side of them empty. Still bewildered with sleep, she turned her head to the left to see Jack in the next seat, glaring down at her and looking as if he might have been doing so for some time.

'You're awake, then?' Cold. Voice icy, one good eye frozen. 'The late film'll start if we stay much longer. It's *Un Chien Andalou*; we'd better leave before it begins. Wouldn't do to spoil your favourite activity with nightmares.' He snatched up his jacket from the seat in front. 'Our film, on the other hand, was lousy. You'll be pleased to hear you didn't miss a thing. You were snoring.'

Mimi closed her eyes tight for an instant and then opened them purposefully in an effort to come back properly from sleep. Alert again to the physical world, she found herself drenched in Jack's anger as if it were a great wave breaking over her. She was saturated by his bitterness, submerged under his despondency. She could taste his dislike seeping into the corners of her mouth. In self-defence she became a rock, a granite mass, and the wave smashed itself uselessly against her, disintegrating into harmless droplets, dispersing and losing its power in the face of her grey implacability.

'Let's go,' she said, reaching under the seat for her bag and standing up.

'Sure you wouldn't like another five minutes to catch up on your beauty sleep?'

'Fuck you,' Mimi said wearily, feeling all of her forty-six years and more, and turned her back on him, walking the whole length of the row to the right-hand aisle, instead of waiting to follow him along the three tipped-up seats to the nearest exit.

Turning right at the row-end would have returned her to the main door out into the foyer, the way they always left this cinema, the way Jack had gone. To maintain her momentum of separateness Mimi turned left when she reached the aisle and walked down the incline towards the green exit-light beside the screen. She pressed down the emergency door's metal bar and let herself into a cold, badly lit, concrete corridor. Presumably, this exit was required by fire regulations; it was too stark to have been intended for general use.

The path was mystifying. It turned senselessly several times in both directions, and there were a couple of short flights of stairs leading downwards. Mimi, whose inability to navigate the city streets with an A–Z so irritated Jack, soon lost her bearings. It was impossible to grasp where the corridor was finally leading. The cinema was small, and, she had thought, built on level ground. Neither the corners she turned nor the stairs she descended seemed reasonable. Still, she followed the route, not wanting to turn back, and eventually she came to a sturdy metal door. With a heave Mimi found herself outside in the night.

She was in a large, empty, concreted area at the back of the cinema. At the far end, she could just see in the gloom, was an alleyway which presumably came out into Camden Town. It was a dead space, four square, flanked by the backs of buildings – the cinema, a supermarket, shops on their public façades – blind brick for the most part with a few functional doors leading out to black metal fire escapes. The only use for this space, as far as Mimi could see, was to store massive galvanized steel containers into which the cinema owners and shopkeepers threw their rubbish at the end of the working day or night. Apart from a feeble exterior light outside the cinema's back exit, the area was in darkness. Mimi surveyed the bleak space in which she found herself, her throat and upper chest constricted with the knowledge that this was not a good situation for a solitary woman to be in after dark. Camden Town at night, even among the bright lights of the High Street, had a slightly dangerous feel to it. People coming out of restaurants and cinemas picked their way around the weaving drunks and shuffling homeless. The last time she was here at night, she was warned as she left a café: 'Take care, it's a jungle out there tonight.' It wasn't New York, but it was a place of evident discrepancy, and required a certain willed blindness on the part of everyone moving through it. Those who could afford to offered coins against the dumb and not-so-dumb resentment they encountered.

Mimi's own different resentment had landed her in this even bleaker hinterland of Camden Town. She took the measure of the distance between her and the dubious looking alleyway that would get her out into what now seemed the security of the High Street, and started to walk towards the far end, flinching at the clip of her footsteps in the uncitylike silence, but, mindful of the importance of appearing confident should anyone be watching her from the shadows, she tried to keep a steady, ordinary pace. Half-way across, at the sight of a lumpy shadow on the ground beside one of the rubbish containers to her left, her worked-for self-assurance drained. She could see nothing of it except that it was a bundle the size of a person and unmoving, but the sudden knowledge that she was not alone in this place, and had not been all along, was arresting. She stopped in mid-stride, and gasped out her shock. But almost instantly, in urgent panic, her body insisted on moving and moving fast – not running, that would draw too much attention to her – past the dormant hulk. She had no further concern about invisible presences lurking in the shadows, about to spring out at her; Mimi's single aim now was to get past the visible reality of the immobile shadow without disturbing its apparent ignorance of her.

It was only when she had passed it and was just a few steps from the alleyway that Mimi considered the possibility that the humped shadow, which she had no doubt was a person, might be in need of help. Though there was still the alleyway to negotiate, the new thought of walking away and leaving behind her someone sick or even dying gripped her. Against her will, which desired only to get into a public space, and every charged nerve fibre in her body, she and the ominous bundle changed roles. *It* became the victim she had been, and *she* the cause of suffering. Everything innate in her, dedicated from prehistory to the cause of survival, said keep going, get out of this dark, dangerous place. London streets were full of sleeping forms, huddled against walls or in doorways. Even in the deepest of winter passers-by made the assumption that they were all right – or as all right as it was possible to be under the circumstances. It would not be reasonable to put herself at risk. No one at this time, in this city, would realistically expect it.

But there was a diminutive portion of herself, something perhaps a little less ancient and at this moment decidedly more inconvenient than the part which knew she should run, that required her to pause. It nagged insistently at her to do what instinct told her was ridiculous, and retrace her steps, back into the lurking shadows to make sure the somnolent body, a person not a bundle now, was not in distress and in need of assistance. She shook her head stubbornly against the idea of going back, but even as she did so, Mimi turned, still disbelieving she could do what she was in fact doing, and walked back the way she had come.

On tiptoe she approached the inert figure, and peered down. All there was to see was a dark, uneven hump of thick, furry material covered at either end with bits of sacking over what she assumed were the head and feet. There was no movement, no sign of life. Mimi stooped to look for any indication that the bundle was breathing. She would have settled for the smallest movement, any rising and falling that the naked eye could perceive, allowing it to put her mind at rest and leave her conscience at that. But there was nothing, and nothing for it (apart from racing for the alleyway) but to investigate further. Narrowing her eyes to slits against the prospect of what she might see, she lifted a corner of the sacking at the end she judged to be the head.

Half a face, the part not concealed by shrouding rags and matted clumps of hair, was visible. The mouth gaped as if frozen in the process of calling for help. The lips were deeply cracked and dry like paper; the skin of the one visible cheek was mottled with scabrous patches, and blue and black in parts, a mixture of bruising and filth. Still uncertain if the tramp was alive, Mimi knelt down closer, and heard a slight rasping noise in the throat which told her she was not looking at a corpse, but made it clear, too, that it was not in a harmless state of sleep. Such breathing as there was was too shallow and sounded wrong, and the stillness was too still to be mistaken for a body at rest. Then the stink of it hit Mimi's nostrils and she had to stand up to reach some clearer air to stop herself from retching.

More than ever her old instinct told her to get away, not from the danger now, but from a diseased and broken specimen to which a healthy creature would give wide berth, refusing to recognize any semblance of connection with itself. But more than ever the smaller, slightly less antiquated portion of herself demanded she acknowledge a sentient being in trouble and do the minimum to provide what help she could. Though her guts, heaving with disgust, urged her to leave this sick, foul creature to continue its decline, it was not quite possible.

She ran into the alleyway and out on to the High Street, failing to notice that she had achieved what she had wanted to do in the first place. She pushed past the cinema queue buying tickets for the late show, and told the man behind the counter to call an ambulance. Then she went back to the inert body in the dark to wait for help to arrive. She stood beside her charge, watching over it, but she did not stand too close, or look again at the face of the comatose creature for whom she had summoned help. She waited with her back to it, looking towards the alleyway and listening for the sound of an ambulance, the imminent arrival of which kept her safe from all she had feared while standing alone in the same darkness just a few minutes before.

When it arrived, a uniformed man and woman heaved their

patient on to a stretcher, preparing to carry it to their vehicle which had been unable to negotiate the alleyway.

'OK, we'll take it from here,' the man said, as Mimi followed them out into the High Street.

They reached the ambulance and slid the stretcher through the open back doors.

'You don't know her name, I suppose?' the man asked Mimi.

Mimi was surprised at the question; why would she? She shrugged her shoulders to indicate she had no idea who the tramp was. The ambulance woman squatted down beside her patient inside the vehicle and looked at the battered, anonymous face with something like compassion through dark, bright eyes that spoke of Mediterranean parentage, though her accent, when she spoke, was pure South London.

'Bella!' she said decisively. She pressed her bunched fingertips to her lips and, opening them like the petals of a flower towards the patient on the stretcher, let the kiss fly. '*Bellissima!*' she cried in an operatically accented parody of her ancestral tongue.

'I don't suppose anyone's ever called her beautiful in her whole life,' Mimi said, moved by the idea of bestowing such a name on the hapless creature.

The man shut the back doors of the ambulance on the patient and his colleague, and climbed into the front seat. Mimi ran up to the driver's window before they drove off.

'Where will you take her?' she asked.

'The Royal Free,' the driver told her.

As Mimi walked away down the High Street she couldn't imagine why she'd asked.

2

NFA. No fixed abode. A derelict.

This much was known: the patient was comatose, female and elderly. Sores on the exposed parts of her body and other signs, such as the pronounced ridges on her nails showed she was also severely malnourished. An upper respiratory infection had moved into her lungs, where pneumonia had probably set in, which would be the direct cause of her coma. There was no indication of who she was.

Two young nurses pulled back the curtains of the cubicle and groaned at the sight of their patient, even though they had on white paper hygiene suits and masks to save them from contracting God knew what. Both young women were familiar with the nightly parade in Accident and Emergency. Torn and bleeding victims of violence. Sudden death in the early hours accompanied by the bemused and disbelieving relatives, distraught lovers, parents or survivors who needed a difficult mixture of realism and comfort. Children whose fevers were not just the touch of 'flu their parents had hoped. The old, the dispossessed, the drunk, the drugged. The natural hallucinators high and desperate on their own brain chemistry. The suicides who find three o'clock in the morning too far from the light of day. Nonetheless, Anna and Cath sighed at having to deal with a comatose baglady, found by a passer-by who thought it would be doing her a favour to keep her life going, instead of letting her slip peacefully away.

She was a bundle of filth and sickness who may or may not live, but Anna and Cath had to tend her, strip away the corruption, and prepare her – make her accessible and reasonably decent – for the doctors to keep her alive. Cath thought women were always worse. Vagrant men seemed more remote from her own existence. It was something about the moment when the last garment had been stripped off to reveal the breasts and vulva. With women, whatever their condition, there were recognizably those parts of the body which for Cath were so private that they could only remind her of herself. Of course, she undressed and bathed other female patients in all kinds of conditions, but mostly they were known to somebody. The female derelicts came in and seemed at first to be beyond gender and personality – and then their bodies would reveal them to have been someone once, a woman once, born, bleeding, bearing, feeding. But they had to be made ready for the doctors' detailed examination and fit to lie with other patients in a bed in a hospital ward. It was her job.

To begin with, it was a matter of identifying and unwrapping the layers in which the body underneath was swathed. Anna and Cath snapped on protective rubber gloves, rolling their eyes and giggling at the awfulness of the task facing them. Cath scissored the coarse string that held the whole horrible bundle together, then they stood back trying to assess where and how to start, and to put off for a moment the reek that would hit them as soon as they began work.

'I wonder what her name is?' Cath said. It was easier to treat – to think of – people as human beings, whatever state they were in and even if they were unconscious, if you had a name for them. At the moment, what they had in front of them might have been a parcel of decaying meat left out of the fridge too long. Even the face was swaddled in rags, and what could be seen of it was so greyed and grimed it was hard to make out any features. It was a bloated face that had suffered violence both from its owner and from others. The nose had been broken at some time, the lips were swollen and cracked and a large bruise on one cheek was reaching its purple climax.

'The paramedics named her Bella,' Anna said. 'I suppose it was a joke, but they've put it on her notes.'

Cath grimaced, and then sighed down at the patient whom they

8

could no longer avoid getting to grips with. 'OK, Bella, my beauty,' she muttered grimly, pushing a stray wisp of hair back under the hood of her suit, 'let's get you sorted.'

The top layer was almost incomprehensible. It comprised the right sleeve, much of the right side of the front, and an uneven two-thirds of the back of an old, synthetic fur coat. Even with gloves Anna and Cath's lips curled in distaste behind their paper masks as, tip-fingered and arms' length, they manoeuvred it off. For all the artificiality of the thick, dark-brown nylon fabric, it had the quality of a dead animal, fur ripped and rotted, and surely harbouring all manner of parasitic life. Cath held open a large plastic sack, extending it as far from her body as she could, while Anna dropped the mangy beast in. Underneath were layers of filthy, torn vests, blouses, skirts, dresses in no very specific order, and a bra which was several strata above her bare flesh; all of it stained and stinking of urine and excrement.

Little noises of disgust came from both young women as they heaved Bella's motionless bulk this way and that to undo buttons and zips that had likely been done up for decades.

'It'd be easier if we used the scissors,' Anna suggested. 'It's not as if we'll be saving this stuff for her to wear again.'

It went quicker after that, snipping through each layer and pulling the remnants off Bella without having to move her about so much.

It reminded Anna, as they got closer and closer to the core of the bundle, of when she was small and her parents had moved house. For weeks they had stripped off old wallpaper. With every layer, a different family, another world had emerged as each new pattern was revealed. Spots and stripes and flocks. People she'd never known; probably dead already before she was born, but coming quite real for Anna as the designs they'd chosen to cover their walls appeared. She had wondered what their names were, just as she had with Bella, and was sorry to be stripping them away rather than adding another layer of her own to the history of the house. It seemed wrong, like bulldozing a cemetery or something. Why couldn't they add their own choice of wall-covering over the top of them all? But her father had said, you've got to do these things properly; strip it down to the plaster, back to the original wall and prepare the surface from scratch. If a job's worth doing . . .

Bella's layers had history in them, too .The clothes came from different periods, though not in the orderly progression of the walls in Anna's childhood home. There were no aesthetic considerations about Bella's layers; they were a jumble of found and donated stuff pulled on only for protection and warmth. Except, Anna wondered, maybe the one nearest to her skin. Perhaps, that first layer had started off as pretty clothes put on by a pretty girl for the pleasure they gave her and others. But with Bella lying there on the trolley, it was an impossible conceit to sustain, beyond reasonable imagination. Still, Anna's humanity insisted, she hadn't been born that way. No one was. Once, she must have been something else.

Finally, Anna and Cath had a full sack which they tied firmly shut, ready for the incinerator, and Bella was exposed. Naked as the day she was born, said Anna. Naked, it struck Cath, as perhaps she hadn't been since before Anna and Cath were born.

The stench was incredible, as if her foul-smelling rags had served to mask the far worse stink of a human body in the process of living decay. She was covered with filth, ulcerations and sores which wept evil-smelling pus. A veritable farmyard of lice grazed over her, herds specializing in her pubic and head hair, and body lice roaming wild. As well as the only-to-be-expected scabies, various fungal conditions colonized the dark, secret places on her body, adding their own special aroma to the fetid air which suddenly hit the two nurses.

Anna and Cath stopped work and stared in dismay at the newly revealed and naked Bella, not shocked in their capacity as nurses, but as young women taking in the extraordinary and terrible possibility that fresh, strong, healthy bodies like their own could ever come to such an end. Neither said anything, but both were making ill-considered bargains with the future to ensure that whatever had happened to Bella's life should not happen to them.

*

10

'OK, Bella, my beauty, let's get you sorted.' The name, then the sound and vibration of scissors snipping at the string around her middle. When the string snapped there was a general loosening. A nasty moment of panic passed as the severing of the string, which Bella feared was all that had held her together, did not result in a collapse into formlessness. She was relieved to find that her substance, once released, didn't dissolve into a seeping, viscous mess, as she had expected, though she waited for another moment, to be quite convinced that she wasn't oozing lava-like down the sides and legs of the trolley. Who could be expected to know what such an experience might feel like? She supposed she had remained in one piece; her unveilers did not run screaming from the room. Everything so far must be staying more or less in place.

So, now I'm being unwrapped, Bella observed. She also noted that they had called her Bella. It seemed for the time being to be as good a name as any, so she decided to accept it, though it was a *fait accompli* since it was already a Bella doing the noting. It *was* her name, after all. An incredible coincidence to have come up with the right name out of so many possibilities. Millions and millions to one, the odds must be, but she had no doubt now that her name was Bella. Always had been, always would be.

She was grateful not to have exuded away into a syrupy puddle on the floor, and pleased to have recovered her name, but more than anything she was excited by the investigation the nurses were making of her. She had no idea what they would find, no recollection of any past, nor any identity beyond the retrieval of her first name. Bella was eager to know what they would make of her. She gathered that the outer layers told Cath and Anna very little, other than that for a long time Bella had been no one very much at all to anyone in the world, including herself. She thought she remembered being no one very much at all, possibly for quite a long time.

She willed them on in their process of discovery. Go deeper, find out more. Find out who she was and where she had come from and where she was going. Go on, pull all that stuff off, cut through the layers, get down to it, girls.

Bella had the unfamiliar and so, for her, remarkable sensation of feeling the air hit her body. She had experienced cold, of course, and, less often, heat in a generalized whole-body way, but she had no memory of what it was like to have nothing between her skin and the air of the world. The shock of the moment of exposure briefly overcame her natural interest in the discoveries they were all about to make. To be naked, after so long, was like being born out of the warmth and protection of the womb, into the cold, unbounded air of life. Shocking.

Once the final layer of clothing had come off, and the shock of flesh-nakedness had passed, Bella became a little impatient at having to wait for the revelations to begin as the nurses paused for inner strength at the sight of her newly uncovered body. Give them time, Bella told herself, they're only young. And soon, though hardly soon enough for Bella, warm, soapy water and a rough flannel were sloughing off the dirt of decades, and eventually they were down to the unadorned, unbesmirched, though admittedly not so healthy, flesh.

Anna was rubbing at Bella's lips as gently as she could with the wet flannel to get the encrustations off, when, as though the water had lubricted them unstuck, they parted very slightly. From some cavernous place deep inside Bella's torso, a croaking, rasping, not-male-nor-female growl escaped through the narrow slit between her lips. Anna let out a shriek and leapt back in fright.

'Ohhhh,' it groaned, like a dirge.

Anna and Cath froze. Bella had not opened her eyes or moved; she seemed as dead to the world as a moment before, except for the moan that had come from her like a ventriloquist without a dummy. Anna shook her head, wide-eyed, mystified. Cath bent over her now silent patient and with only a slight hesitation, gently stroked her temples as she spoke reassuringly.

'It's all right, Bella.'

The two nurses waited, but nothing else happened. Bella had

not regained consciousness, they were certain.

Oh, can't you just get on? She had heard the grumbling voice, too, and was as much surprised by it as the nurses, but it wasn't as interesting to her as the vivid and urgent project of the uncovering of herself. She tried to be composed, as a good comatose patient should be, but her desire to get to the nub of things was almost too strong to bear.

At last, however, her waiting was rewarded and she felt the unmistakable sensation of a scalpel scoring an incision across her scalp. The line of the cut ran laterally over her cranium from ear to ear, then down each side of her neck and shoulders, cutting across the top of her arms like a sleeveless blouse, and continuing down both sides of her torso, to the top of her thighs.

Ahh, now we're getting down to it.

With consummate skill, Anna and Cath gently peeled the epidermal layer forward from Bella's scalp, pulling it down her forehead, and carefully lifted the skin and flesh away from her face. Once this tricky manoeuvre had been accomplished, the rest of the flesh came away easily from neck, breast, and belly. This time, the girls didn't stop for a breather, but got on with the job with an efficiency Bella found admirable. An electric saw whined up to speed and began to cut a frontal section through the thick skull bone, then whizzed around the rib cage until it was detached so that the nurses, bless them, were able to lift the freed sections of bone clear away. Finally, here was all there was of Bella to be seen.

It was not easy for Bella to know where to start her detailed survey of herself, faced with the gorgeous, technicoloured feast below. The overall mêlée of shape and texture held her momentarily mesmerized as her gaze slid over and around the smooth and slippery curves, erratic coils, ruffled fronds, fatty shape-defying clumps. A multihued confusion at first glance, but everything within a red/brown/pink/beige colour spectrum, and all of it lubricated, wet and glistening.

Bella could have stared down at herself for an eternity, but she

13

felt some formal recognition of this meeting with the very centre of herself was called for, so she disciplined her gaze to locate the brain which sat, elaborately wrinkled and throbbing softly like a car ticking over, a pleasantly pinkish grey, in the cup of the remaining portion of her skull.

'Hello, Bella,' she said to her brain, giving it pride of place in her identity. 'How are you?'

It was a silly question because for all its gentle pulsing and rosy appearance, Bella knew it wasn't all that well. It hardly could be, since its body was lying unconscious on a hospital trolley. Still, politeness cost nothing, even though, disappointingly, there was no obvious response. But then she had another thought and dropped her eyes down to her chest cavity where the heart pumped ploddingly away.

'Hello, Bella,' she said to her heart, just in case. 'How are you?'

A veritable twang of pleasure reverberated around the veins and arteries leading to and from Bella's oversized and weary pump at being greeted so directly. Her heart-strings hummed like a harp at receiving such recognition, and Bella was delighted to get a response.

But who knew where one properly addressed the centre of oneself? She had no recollection of being offered such information in her past – although her memory of any past at all was, at best, foggy, so she may have missed something. There was, however, a faint memory at the back of her mind of a story about a fairy not invited to a christening and causing all kinds of trouble as a result of having been overlooked. This thought forced her to drop her gaze further down her torso and bid an uncharitably brisk 'Good evening' to her uterus, ovaries, cervix and vaginal vestibule, which suite of organs, for reasons she failed to recollect, she had no time for at all. Better to be safe than sorry, but surely it was not *that* region in which her very self resided. 'Bella?' she barely articulated, hoping it was hard of hearing and continuing her tour before it had a chance to acknowledge its identity.

In any case, it seemed unfair (and possibly unwise) not to give her lungs the time of day, realizing that without them there would be a sizeable void at the centre of her. She didn't like the look of them at all. Lungs were supposed to be pink and spongy, but large areas of hers were blackened and solid. Now, how did she know what lungs are supposed to be like? For an impressive moment she wondered if she was a doctor in her waking life, but then the word *lights* came into her mind, along with a vision of a butcher's shop. I must have had a cat, she realized, conceding that it was more likely than a doctor's licence.

Then, not wishing to give offence, she bid an initially cautious howdeedo to her intestines, upper and lower, and unexpectedly found herself enchanted by those abdominal regions, a true wonderland of contrasting surfaces, shapes and colour. 'Visceral,' she murmured, gazing with satisfaction on her gleaming kidneys, frilled pancreas and superbly convoluted tubular colon. 'Decidedly visceral.'

She marvelled at pastel labyrinthine coils, as elaborately and intricately packed within its space as the brain, which seemed almost to be a compressed echo of these lower regions. Lying on top, in counterpoint to the complexity beneath, was the irresistibly gleaming, darkly saturated mass of her liver. The need to touch, to stroke it was overwhelming. She found a hand and ran it back and forth across the slippery, red-brown surface, satiny smooth to the touch, her fingertips sliding over the glacial surface like skates slicking over ice.

Yet for all the beauty and strangeness of her insides, and even the humming of her heart-strings, Bella felt she had not yet located whatever it was she was looking for. Herself, as she supposed. She could be anyone – though now at least she was an anyone whose name was Bella and who lay unconscious on a hospital trolley. But as to who she had been, let alone who she was, there was nothing but blankness and anatomy. There was no story of herself at all. It was all very disheartening.

'Bella,' she murmured anxiously, 'where are you?'

Disconsolately, she let her gaze wander away from her liver and back up her torso, past her shoulders and along her neck, where she found what she had omitted from her itinerary. Her flayed, membraneless face was so alien and yet so uncannily beautiful that, as she peered down at it, she saw tears well up from the inner corners of the eye sockets and wash over the skinned orbits. The eyes stared unblinking back up at her, lidless and basilisk blind, tearful at being unable to see the beauty for themselves.

She knew this face to be her own, though no one else who knew her (who knew her?) would have. Stripped of all its flesh, the exposed muscle, veins, arteries and nerves wove intricate patterns around each other to provide a latticework of scaffolding behind the skin no longer there to conceal them. Delicate blood vessels, veins and arteries, with tiny tributaries running off them like tree roots, snaked between and beneath bundles of striated muscle spanning the space between her temple and jaw bones like rope bridges. At either corner of the mouth these muscle groups fanned out like peacock tails, at the service of expression, ready to promote a smile or scowl or any of a hundred demonstrations of mood in between. As well as that curious purpose, the roseate fretwork was designed for practical use: to open and close the mouth so that it might eat, yawn, shout a warning; to manipulate the now absent eyelids enabling alertness or sleep; to suffuse the face and brain with blood for tissue repair and life itself.

But aside from the obvious usefulness of the arrangement, it made a pattern of breathtaking beauty, though not the human beauty which flits around a complete face as the underlying mechanisms create the mobility we generally recognize as beautiful. Without expression, without even a suggestion of its possibility, this face had the cool beauty of architecture or abstract art, and Bella knew it did not tell a truthful tale about how she might have looked in her fully epidermal form. She knew that in all likelihood she was no beauty, and doubted, along with her rescuer, if she ever had been. But with all the life subtracted, she had acquired a monumental and timeless symmetry, a still perfection of form which almost stopped the heart. In that static and impersonal beauty, Bella felt that she could really see her face, what it really was, what she really looked like, at last, and for the first time, now that the effects of time and experience had been stripped away. She hovered over this face of hers, whose frozen, tear-glazed orbits ached up towards their owner, whose still lips rested tensionless against each other, and recognized it.

'Bella,' she whispered, and might have seen the merest shadow of a melancholy smile pass over the skinned face. The face was Bella, but still, Bella was not the face. A face without features offered no story, and above all else it was a story that Bella ached for. She closed her eyes on her anatomy and searched the darkness for something with a narrative. Something fit for a Bella without a past or future.

Mask

It was dusk now, but not yet evening. This was always the worst time for her. He was not back. Dusk was a time of quiet terror. The failing light blued the world beyond the window, and the bright daylight white of the interior walls echoed the shadowy blue-grey outside like a treachery. If she could have, she'd have pulled the blinds and turned on the lights well before dusk set in to strain her heart, but she couldn't go near the windows before complete darkness had made her invisible to passers-by, so, in his absence, there was no alternative but to suffer the twilight and the descending ache.

It was a small price to pay, considering her good fortune. In her condition, she should have been more afraid of daylight than of its fading, but he had taken care of daylight for her. It held no threat, as the waning of the light did, for far less obvious reason. Yet Bella welcomed the complete darkness, when it had come. It was her friend. She tried to see dusk as its precursor, but there was something else. She supposed it was the old fear of that which is neither one thing nor the other, and of the danger lurking in the change-over – the possibility that *here* things might get stuck. Twilight was a threat to the cycle of day and night, and she waited now, in the dimming of the light, barely breathing, for dusk to end and for the world to continue turning. Strange that she should care. That fear, from long ago – from childhood (hers and the species) – was at least some connection between herself and the normal world. She supposed she should cherish it. But she didn't, not even now, not even here, from the place of safety he had given her.

Anxiety crawled through her belly and wound its way up,

stopping and solidifying like an indigestible lump in her throat. It was not particularly late. He had come back later than this before. Always come back. Always would, he said. Bella knew it was true, and yet there was invariably the tiny fear scratching around the edges of her mind, that tonight, this night, he wouldn't return. But he always had. After all these months, there was sufficient repetition for her to trust him. He loved her, after all. She didn't doubt that.

She wondered again if she loved him. How could she possibly know, when her very life depended on him? What did it matter, anyway? She wanted him there, with her, to alleviate the growing darkness. Still, still, she told herself, there was no obvious reason to worry. But worry, once it has broken down the door, doesn't dance to the tune of reason. She knew there was no alternative to waiting, but she was also aware that at some point (When? When would that point have arrived?), if he had not returned, she would have to acknowledge to herself that she was alone.

She put the thought out of her mind. It was unthinkable. She tried a trick she had used as a child, when fear that something bad was going to happen crept up on her at night, and there was nothing to be done but wait, and wait and see. On those occasions, she would make herself imagine it was already past the time of the foreseen danger. She would envisage the next morning as if it had arrived, sun up, breakfast on the table, brushing her teeth, washing, getting dressed: everything normal and ordinary. Sometimes, if she mentally skipped in that way over the dangerous night to come, and put herself beyond it into its future, the fear would disappear, like a dream, or a cloud blown by the current of air that brought morning, and then it was as if the danger really had passed.

Now, she imagined as vividly as she could the moment when his key made its particular noise as he inserted it into the lock, his footsteps crossing the threshold, the door banging shut, and him calling out, as he always did: 'It's OK, it's me.' For a moment she was relieved, but the sound of the door and his footsteps were not followed by the projected sound of his voice. Her imagination

19

turned on her and made the fear all the more real. She couldn't make it work properly. She couldn't make the sound of 'It's OK, it's me' ring in her head.

It wasn't until several weeks after the explosion that she had become aware of him. He had been there all along, following the ambulance to hospital on his motorbike. Each morning, before he set about his business, he stopped by to check on her progress, and at the end of his day he returned to the hospital. All this, she didn't learn until much later.

The nurses got used to him arriving every day to ask after her, and thinking that the attention of another human being, if not a friend, a concerned stranger who had helped to save her life, might be good for her, they had let him sit for a few minutes each day at her bedside in the side room they allocated to her. Later, she suspected (correctly) that a little bold flirtatiousness may also have helped to promote his cause among the nurses, perhaps with the addition of an occasional gift: a watch, a pair of earrings, salvaged from the back of a lorry.

Once she had come round, there was a great deal of pain, but it was worst and sharpest around her face and neck, and when, after weeks of stillness, she tentatively put her fingers to her cheeks and brow, she felt the starchy weave of bandages.

Her first conscious encounter with him was when she noticed a gigantic, hideously multicoloured vaseful of flowers on her bedside locker. One evening she turned her head as she began to wake from the dreamy doze she had been in – forever, it seemed – and saw the preposterous mass of brilliant orange chrysan-themums, scarlet roses and acid yellow lilies in the fluted hospital vase. For a moment she thought she was hallucinating in horribly hyper-vivid colour, but then she supposed they must have been sent by – she tried to think who might have sent them, but nothing, no name, no face, came to mind. Somehow, she felt, whoever it was who had known her and found her would not have had such bad taste as to send such a blowsy mix-up of overbred specimens.

Luckily, she couldn't speak – not only were the bandages over her face, but her jaws were wired – because she would have said, 'What the fuck is that horror show?', and he was sitting on the other side of the bed.

'Hello,' he said, gruffly.

He had watched her begin to come round and look something like alert for the first time. She turned her head, painfully slowly, towards him. He was wearing jeans, a T-shirt, and a Levi's jacket. He was, to her eyes, a huge man, with a great expanse of chest that was mostly worked-for muscle, but which, one day, would run to fat. His upper arms and thighs bulged inside the denim, and although his big, red-rough hands were hidden in the creases of his elbows as he sat with folded arms, waiting for her to finish looking at him, she knew they would be massive. He had a rather florid complexion, though with a surprisingly angular, wolf-like face. His eyes were a disconcerting, vacant blue; intense in colour, but limpid as they stared at her, like a cloudless Mediterranean sky. She thought later, when she'd had more time and clearer vision, that he was not unattractive in a rough, discordant way, if one was not startled by his size.

'Hello,' he said.

She blinked her question at him.

He looked down at his knees, awkwardly, as if he feared his eyes might show her something other than their colour.

'You won't remember me. I – was with you – before the ambulance came.'

He looked up, worry swimming in his no-longer clear blue eyes, realizing he shouldn't have reminded her. She blinked in a way that was meant to be reassuring enough for him to continue.

'I've been coming to see you.'

They waited together in silence for a little while, until he suddenly slapped his thighs lightly, in a gesture of getting up, and said, 'I'd better be going. Nurse said I wasn't to tire you if you woke up. I'll come back tomorrow.'

And although she didn't doubt his word, she thought no more about him. She was still too ill for extended curiosity.

He came every day to the hospital with his gaudy flowers, and she got stronger as the weeks passed, though, of course, she still couldn't speak.

The nurses gave her a blackboard and chalk with which she could answer questions (Yes, the pain is still bad. No, I don't need a bedpan), and ask for things (Can I have a painkiller? Will there be another operation?).

At first, she didn't question his presence at her bedside. He would sit quietly all evening, and sometimes, hesitantly, take her hand, looking at her to see if her eyes – all there was to see – minded the physical contact. Funnily enough, she didn't mind. She rather enjoyed the feel of his big, rough-skinned hand closed around hers. But still, as she came more and more into reality, she found his presence puzzling.

WHY DO YOU COME HERE? she wrote on her blackboard one evening.

He looked as if he was sitting an exam, and the one question he hadn't revised was the only one on the paper. She tapped twice with her chalk at the words on the blackboard to repeat her question. He drew a deep breath.

'Dunno,' he mumbled, like a dunce being shamed in class.

She took the chalk and drew an impatient circle around the WHY, making her point with a horrible screech that made him wince.

'Got nothing better to do,' he tried, and grinned his best boyish grin at her, the one that won over all the nurses.

She glared her rejection of his answer at him through the bandages, and wiped the board with an impatient swipe of the cloth.

WHY? she wrote again, this time making the word shout for her by filling the whole space of the board with it.

He did not answer. He sat on the hard chair and stared down at his feet. She watched, alarmed, his jaw trembling and his hands clenching and unclenching, making his biceps bulge dangerously, in a caricature of suppressed rage. For a moment, she thought he was going to hit her, and tensed herself, terrified of the added pain she would not be able to protect herself from. It was the moment when she recognized the degree of violence he could

22

summon. His arm, fully wound now, lashed out as expected, and she flinched, giving herself a searing pain, but instead of landing her a blow, he snatched the blackboard and cloth from her hands and roughly wiped away the WHY, throwing the cloth back on the bed, and taking up the chalk. He wrote as if he were carving flesh, using single strokes that he joined together with staccato, jerky movements.

I LOVE YOU appeared with jagged urgency on the board. He stared at it for a moment, and then flung it on the bed into her lap, and, still shaking with unprocessed violence, he slammed out of the room.

When she thought about this moment later, it seemed important to remember the sequence of the thoughts which came to her as she lay propped up on the pillows, and stared at the message on her knees. She knew she could never know for certain. Memory played tricks, and more than that, thoughts do not, in reality, come in single threads to be unravelled and analysed like chromosomes. Perhaps she had a dozen thoughts all at once, and some of them irrelevant, like wondering if she needed to pee. That was probably closest to the truth, but she was uneasy at the possibility of certain thoughts coming first, and others later.

When he declared his love on her blackboard, he knew no more about her than the doctors. He did not even know what she looked like – what she had looked like, what she looked like now – because the first time he saw her, her features were too torn and bloodied to make them out, and since then, her entire face and neck had been swathed in bandages. One reaction she had to his declaration was simple perplexity. How could he love her (and somehow she couldn't doubt the truth of what he wrote, even if, then, she didn't understand its extent) without having seen her face? The problem was not that she imagined herself to be unsightly; there was a covering of bandages. But it was impossible that she should be loved *sight unseen*. How could anyone love another person who was literally without a face? She couldn't even speak. She could not understand what it was that was loved by him. That mystery was to deepen once the bandages were

23

removed, but that was later. At the time of his declaration, she pushed her incomprehension away and focused on what she did understand.

She had a notion of what being loved meant. It meant help, the easement of her life; it might, from now on, mean the very pattern of her continued existence. Never mind about why, or who or how. She knew she had no other answers to her present situation. So she permitted his love for her, and let the anomalies lie together in the dark place where other troubling feelings crouched, ready, but not daring quite to spring.

He had come the next day, as usual, looking nervous but no longer angry. His eyes darted to and from her face with a question, as he stood, just inside the door, with his elbows pressed close to at his sides, hands thrust in his jean's pockets. He waited, ready to be dismissed.

She took the blackboard from the bedside locker and scratched: NO FLOWERS? I LIKE WHITE ONES BEST.

Before she left the hospital, her doctor tried once more to discuss her injuries. He had come several times to her bedside and begun a conversation.

'Bella, we ought to discuss . . .'

She would shake her head and write: FACIAL INJURIES. I KNOW.

She refused to look at herself, although for some weeks her doctor and the nurses waged a campaign to make her confront what had happened to her. Once the bandages came off, they explained gently, sympathetically, it was important she look at herself as she actually was. They had, they told her, gone as far as they could, for the present, with reconstructive surgery. Her face had been virtually rebuilt, but it was only an approximation of what people normally thought of as a face. They didn't say that, of course, but it was clear to her that that was what they meant. She should look at herself, they told her; there had to be a gradual coming to terms with her new looks. They would do more operations, and it would help her know what kind of progress

24

they were making. They were talking about relativity. She wasn't interested. They suggested that nothing could be worse than what she was probably imagining.

NOT IMAGINING ANYTHING, she told them.

His first declaration of love, and her implicit acceptance of it, was never mentioned between them again while she was in hospital. She had asked a question, and received an answer. He had made a statement and she had not responded negatively. That was as far as either of them needed or wanted to go. He came almost every evening to be with her in the hospital during all the weeks of her recovery. He was a solid, unchanging presence – a *regularity* in her unknowable new life. Once or twice a nurse arrived to tell her that he had called to say he wouldn't be able to come that evening. It seemed, by then, perfectly reasonable to both of them that he should let her know if he was going to miss a visit, as if he had an obligation to her that only the most urgent matter allowed him to break. If he had let an evening go by without letting her know he wasn't coming, she would have been beside herself with worry that something had happened to him: there could have been no other explanation.

They talked very little during his visits – not surprisingly since her half of the conversation was conducted with chalk. He seemed perfectly content to sit in silence, though if she questioned him, he gave answers of a sort.

One evening she wrote ARE YOU MARRIED?

He twisted the gold signet ring on his little finger, then held it up for her to see.

'Wife and kids. Two,' he said in a clipped voice.

? she wrote under her original question.

'I don't live there any more. It wasn't anything special. Me and Mary just sort of drifted together. There's nothing to say about it. We went together and she fell for a kid. It's what happens.'

WHEN DID YOU LEAVE HER?

He shifted his chair slightly.

'Not long ago.'

She knew it was the day he had pulled up his motorbike to see if he could help the victims of flying glass, blast and fire after a bomb had exploded accidentally while the bomber, on his way to plant it, had inexplicably stopped in a café for a cup of tea. But he didn't say so, and it was easy for her to leave the chalk lying on the board, and let the silence lengthen.

One day, three months or so after the explosion that had destroyed her face, he arrived with something on his mind.

'I've got a house,' he said. 'It needs doing up, but the doctor said you'll have to be in hospital a few more weeks, so there's time to get it ready.'

It wasn't clear whether it was his house, or if he'd got the use of it. He didn't ask, had never asked her, about family or friends. He had never discussed with her what plans she might have. Now, he was telling her that he'd got somewhere for her to live sorted out, and that he would be taking care of her. She had spent no time wondering what she was going to do when she left the hospital. She knew she wouldn't be returning to her life, but she hadn't given a moment's thought to how, exactly, she was going to live. His announcement came as no surprise. She had, she realized, been waiting for it. It seemed perfectly natural that he should have made the arrangements, and that she would leave the hospital in his care. There were no questions she wanted to ask.

GOOD, she wrote on her blackboard.

The house that he had made for her was situated in a quiet back street of a small country town. Every room in it – her safe house, as she had come to think of it – was painted white and furnished only with what was necessary. He had made it exactly as she wanted it. In the hospital, he had brought her catalogues and showed her magazines, and they had gone through them together while she shook her head at flounces, patterns, and lively colours, and nodded at things so undecorated he would have passed them over without pausing if she had not put her hand over his as it made to turn the page. He wasn't impressed with her taste, but the house was for her; it had to be the way she wanted it.

They had planned the house that he was creating for her

without reference to any kind of future. It was accepted by then that she would live there when she left hospital, and it was also assumed, without either of them discussing it, that he would live there too, but that he would not be living *with* her, as it were. Such elaborations of understanding were achieved precisely because they had no conversations about their plans. The unspoken went on working for her.

He called the house their hideaway. It was a joke, because it *was* a hideaway for both of them, as she knew, though what his reasons were for needing one she chose not to explore. That he loved her, she was in no doubt. Adored her. It was improbable, but obviously true nevertheless. She came to understand that she had brought some part of him into being which loved her for giving it life. It was an aspect of him that knew nothing of the other him, she suspected, the one who went about his unthinkable daily life outside the house. Perhaps, in some way, his two aspects remained strangers to each other, living in different sectors, a daytime and an evening self. Sometimes she imagined him like the cycling of the planet. Do day and night themselves know nothing of each other?

He, of course, had breathed life into her in a much more literal way than she had into him. She owed him everything; every moment she had of continued existence, of future, was because of what he had done for her. But still, she could not say whether she loved him, or what she felt about him, except for the simple, inescapable fact that he was her whole life. She couldn't analyse her feelings beyond that. It was better not to.

But they had embarked on an adventure together, and during those months in the house they had slipped the noose of time – her, entirely; him, when he was there. Most evenings, in her house, her place of safety, when she believed she had no more to fear than the twilight, he came back at around eight. He would smile as he came through the door of her room and immediately go to the windows to deal with the blinds.

'I've done the others,' he'd say, to let her know that she could go downstairs now.

The house, in its back street, was all stillness, even during the day. The sound of shoes walking on the pavement occasionally rang out in the silence. The chatter of a couple as they walked by reverberated in the quiet road, as if a sleepy dreamer were being shaken back to waking. During the day she lived in a pool of silence. He had offered her a radio or TV for her room, but she had said no. Sometimes, before he came home, she could imagine the world wiped away, with her the only survivor.

There was only one mirror in the house. It was for him when he shaved. Initially, he tried to do without one. For the first few days he arrived in her room with the morning tea with nicks and scratches on his face and neck, and small areas of cheek and chin that still showed untouched bristle. He had a thick, fast-growing beard.

She wrote on the pad beside the bed: YOU CAN'T GO OUT LIKE THAT.

He grinned nervously at the direction the conversation was tending.

'I'll grow a beard,' he said, trying to close the topic before they had to confront the source of the problem.

She shook her head. He was not the sort of person to wear a beard, and she suspected it would not be appropriate in his life out in the world.

GET A MIRROR, she wrote on the pad. He winced slightly at the word and tore the sheet off, crushing it in his fist.

'It's all right, I'll get used to it.'

But the following day, when he brought her tea, there was a stamp-sized piece of toilet paper stuck to the underside of his jaw, saturated and bright red with the blood that still oozed from his torn skin.

GET A MIRROR! she wrote with an emphatic full stop that broke the tip of her pencil.

He kept it in the bathroom cabinet.

Nothing more was said after her insistent note, but the following morning he came into her room properly shaved and with no new nicks among the old scratches that were already

28

beginning to heal. After he left, she went to the bathroom to wash and noticed that the key, which was usually left in the lock of the cabinet above the basin, was missing. When she tried the door, it wouldn't open. She looked around the bathroom, but apart from the cabinet itself there was only the bath, toilet and washbasin. There were no places to hide things, except for the cistern, which she checked, but there was nothing there. She thought, perhaps, he had taken it with him, but it would have been awkward, having to remember to transfer the key from suit to suit, and to find it in the morning before he got dressed. She stood on tiptoe and felt blindly along the top edge of the cabinet with her fingers. She strained her fingertips forward, and her toes upward as far as they would go – she was not tall – and finally reached what she was looking for. She manoeuvred the key carefully towards her, and, when she had it in her grasp, tried it in the lock of the cabinet. It fitted, and when she turned it, she felt the metal bar retract and release the door. She did not open it, but turned the key back in the opposite direction and replaced it on top of the cabinet. She didn't take it down again for a long time, though she reached up every morning to make sure he hadn't moved it. The mirror was there, and she knew how to get it if she should want to.

She hadn't seen her face since he had rescued her. The windows of the house were all hung with muslin so she couldn't catch her reflection on those evenings when he came back late. She made doubly sure by keeping the lights off until he had blanked out the windows. There was nothing else reflective in the house (except for the mirror in the bathroom cabinet). No shiny metal kitchenware. All the saucepans were ceramic, as was the sink, and the utensils were made of wood or mat black plastic. These were not matters he had discussed with her. He bought the kitchen equipment himself, able to guess by then the kinds of things she would like, but neither of them ever mentioned the dissonant fact that they ate and drank with plastic cutlery and tumblers. She understood at their first meal that the white plastic knives and spoons were to protect her from accidentally seeing herself, as she could not have avoided doing in the bright, stainless-steel bowls and planes of regular cutlery.

Bella was glad she knew where the mirror, and the key to it, was, but she was not yet ready to look into it, nor certain if she ever would be.

He's not coming back, Bella thought with sudden certainty. This was the night when the silence would endure, when it would not be broken by the sound of him coming home. Night had fallen now, and even though he had come home later once or twice, she knew that the morning would come and he would still not be here. Nor ever again. Something had happened and he couldn't get back to her. Real life had caught up with him. Where had he got the money for the house? Or he might simply have decided not to return, to get back to an old life, or start another new one. Had she recovered too much, had she become too flesh-real the night he brought her the mask?

It didn't matter what the reason was. The reason disappeared along with him. She was alone and in the dark. She knew he wouldn't be back.

3

The windows of the flat were dark as Mimi arrived home from the cinema, and the car was not in front of the house. Mimi was not surprised by Jack's absence, though familiarity, in this case, conferred no sense of security, but only the re-emergence of a deadening weight inside her, as if something indigestible eaten previously was once again making itself felt. The repetition of symptoms added to her immediate discomfort the more generally discomforting knowledge that the cause had not and would not go away.

It was eleven-thirty; reasonably late enough, she decided, to go to bed. Anyone might, but perhaps not someone who had just spent an hour or more asleep in the cinema. In recognition of this she took a Valium, though in tonight's circumstances – the sick tramp, the car gone – she would have taken one anyway. She urgently wanted to be asleep.

Sleep and its effects had always been an important part of Mimi's life. As a child she had suffered terrible nightmares. She'd wake sweating and screaming, shaken awake by her mother. It might have helped if she could have told her mother what she had been dreaming about, but her nightmares were without any narrative capable of telling. They never had a story, just atmosphere. Night after night Mimi struggled to be released from an existence in which she was under threat, though from what, she never knew. The looming danger, the horror of its inevitability and, worse, its namelessness, terrorized her. Her young sleep dripped with something malevolent and lurking, from which she couldn't be rescued because it was never defined.

Without a dream world there was not even the dream hope of summoning help. The fear was absolute, and there was no escaping it while she slept. The horror was in the anticipation of a certainty, not the discomfort of suspense. With suspense there was at least the possibility of a good outcome. In Mimi's dreams (if that was the right word for something which was not more than ambience) no good outcome was remotely possible.

But the nightmare phase had passed, as the doctor to whom her mother took her said it would.

'Just give her a cup of hot cocoa and a cuddle,' he advised. 'She'll grow out of them. It's a difficult process, growing up. Perhaps, that's what's frightening her.'

Mimi's mother asked if her daughter ought to be 'seeing someone for her nerves'.

'I think she'd be more in need of a psychiatrist if she wasn't frightened of growing up. I'm still frightened of it myself,' he said with a smile.

Had she been afraid to grow up as the doctor had said? Mimi wondered now, sitting in bed, sipping cocoa, waiting for the Valium to start working. She thought he may have been right. The great blanking wall of fear that loomed over her and threatened to engulf her while she slept might very well have been the future she dreaded. As a child, the future seemed as blank as her nightmares. She remembered walking through the streets, on her way to school, or shopping with her mother, and scrutinizing every woman she passed, wondering of each: will I be like that? Or that? And will a ten-year-old girl pass me on the streets when I'm an older woman of thirty and wonder will she be like me? But there was no picture of herself as a woman of thirty, no sense of what such a person might be. She had not even the vaguest notion of who she might become, though her school friends did about their futures. They seemed to have themselves mapped out, not just their future plans – career, marriage, children, nice old age with aforementioned children taking care and loving them – but actually *who they were*, as if it were a thing already known, a route already determined, and all they had to do was carry on and grow into the selves which were waiting for them up ahead. For Mimi the future was nothing but blankness. None of the women she passed on the street seemed to be what she might become. Becoming *anything* was unimaginable, no matter how hard she tried to imagine it. When, occasionally, she saw tramps, they seemed, if they were women, to be as likely candidates for her future as any respectable North London matron pushing a glassy black pram proudly in front of her. She would wonder if the tramps and drunks might not have been ten years old once, and knew they must have been. And had they, too, once peered into adults' faces as they passed and been unable to fit themselves into their future?

She remembered tonight's tramp. Ten years old once. Then twenty, then thirty. Who had she been, before she became her future? Quite possibly her future was now at an end and she would just never wake from her coma. Would she want that? What was there to come round for? Mimi wondered if she had done her tramp a favour by getting help. She had looked, Mimi remembered, like no one, or anyone. She could have been anyone who had wandered through the story of their life and come to its conclusion. She was as anonymous as the women Mimi had peered at as a child, wondering if she might become such a person. The unknown distance trod between the tramp's conclusion and her absent story gave Mimi a vertiginous sense that she might, for all Mimi could fathom, have been someone she had once known. Storyless spaces, like black holes, suck ferociously on whatever comes into their orbit in their need to be occupied. In Mimi's experience only her childhood nightmares were content to exist without being filled in. It was the absence of an intervening story that suggested to Mimi the possibility that the tramp could have been someone known to her, not anything about her that jogged Mimi's memory.

Mimi distrusted memory. In the first, and most obvious, place, it was unreliable. A picture came to Mimi's mind's eye. A tableau from her childhood: a frozen vision of herself, her father and her mother standing on a street in London. It represented a real moment, a fragment of her history which she had no doubt had happened, but it was fatally flawed as a memory, because when Mimi examined the picture her remembering eye painted in the present, she saw that the image was from the point of view of someone who was observing from several feet above and behind the event. A *fourth* someone who was not her since Mimi could not possibly have seen at the time *three* people, two tall, one small. A real memory, whatever that was, would have been a picture from the child's – her – point of view, yet she saw the child, too, from above and behind. The memory, therefore, was a contrivance, a picture created after the event, and with no more verisimilitude than any other fiction. Which brought her to the other reason for distrusting memory. While it was true that she could experience the anxiety and disappointment of the young child whom Mimi saw pictured between the two adults, as if the moment had happened yesterday, she knew that the child in her memory was not *her*, and the emotions she felt as the picture stood before her eyes were those anyone might imagine feeling under such circumstances. It was not even that the child was *no longer* her. The divorce was more profound than that. She allowed that the child had existed, and even that she continued to exist in her own right, in the past, lodged inside Mimi's mind, but there was no umbilical connection between them. The events the picture recalled may have happened, and she might even feel the *kind* of feelings the child felt at the time, because of the artfulness of memory, but it did not bring that child, frozen in time, and her present imagining self any closer together. Memory was therefore pointless, nullified as anything other than a story, with no more personal truth than any other fantasy. The past was another territory, a land apart in time and space, and those who inhabited it were separate individuals belonging only in their period. They had had their reality, made their mark in their own time, but like persistent ghosts eternally hungering for substance, they wanted to stay, to impress themselves on the world in spite of their non-existence. Memory was the phantoms of a dead past which refused to let go and be still. The child had *not* grown and developed into the person who was Mimi. She had stopped in time and remained forever a child locked into the what happened of then. A person might choose to maintain the false connection and give themselves an alibi for mood and behaviour, but it was, had to be, a choice.

That things had happened in the past, she couldn't deny. The pull of old re-animated events gave memories a spurious power, but their apparent value was false. Cheap tinsel memories, good ones or bad, were like looking at an old film. It was a seductive pastime, watching flickering images that seemed to project a continuity, and a complete story. In reality there were only discrete moments, like frames of a film, which her mind, hankering as mortal minds were set to do, after connection, spliced together and ran through its projector. The images and feelings attempted to suck her in, trying to convince her that her present existence was nothing more than the sum of her past. This was nonsense, of course, because memories were unverifiable, absent shadows, and all the more treacherous for being covered with emotions, like slime, that stuck unbelonging to the owner of the observing eye.

The picture which had beamed on to her inner screen nevertheless persisted.

'Wait here, Miriam. Don't move. Understand? Just stand here and wait.'

'Where are you going?' the ten-year-old child asked, alarmed at her mother's tone of voice.

'Never you mind. Don't move!'

Miriam watched her mother turn and walk back the way they had just come. She scanned the area carefully, but saw no one she recognized. Miriam's mother crossed the road at the lights and stopped at the wide stone steps leading up to St Martin's-in-the-Fields. After a moment, she climbed them and disappeared through the dark entrance to the church. She didn't turn back to check on her daughter two hundred yards away, standing on the pavement outside South Africa House. Miriam's main anxiety left her. Her father couldn't be in there, not in a church. For a moment, she relaxed.

They were on one of their treks through central London, Miriam and her mother, in search of Miriam's father. Leah would work up a special fury every so often and pull a coat on her daughter, saying, 'We're going to find that bastard, and when I get to him . . .' She didn't have to say what she would do. Her mother had kept a large, sharp kitchen knife in her capacious handbag ever since her husband had walked out on her. 'In case I ever see him on the street,' she explained to Miriam. 'I'll swing for him yet, believe you me.'

One day when they were walking up Charing Cross Road, Leah saw Miriam's father, Ray, coming towards her. Miriam hadn't noticed him, but her mother's radar was sharply tuned. Miriam heard her mother screech 'Come here, you pig!' and turned to see her pull the knife from her bag. For a frozen moment Miriam followed the direction of the knife's tip with her eyes and saw her father standing a few feet in front of them staring in horror at his wife's twisted face and the blade gleaming in her hand. He turned and bolted in the opposite direction, ducking down the stairs at Leicester Square tube station. His deserted wife followed him underground, brandishing her weapon and shrieking for the bastard to stop and let her kill him, while, along with other mystified or amused onlookers, Miriam stood at the entrance and waited to see what was going to happen. She imagined them running along the platform and beyond it into the tunnel, certain that her mother's fury would give her the edge of speed to catch up and get within a knife's thrust of him. Miriam thought that for that moment before he ran, her father had caught her eye. But she wasn't sure; it couldn't have been for more than a split second if he had.

Curious onlookers peered down into the underground to see if anything interesting had happened. Miriam remained where she was. Most people seemed entertained by the drama. Miriam hated most people.

Ever since he left, she had prayed at night, with the gleaming knife in mind, that they wouldn't ever bump into her father in the street, or anywhere. She hoped he was a long way away. She didn't know what would happen to her if her mother killed her father, but she didn't doubt she would kill him if she got the chance. She wished her father hadn't left, but then she'd remember how scared she'd been that they might kill each other when they were living together, so perhaps it was better that he had gone. Sometimes she wished she'd gone with him, but she didn't know where he'd gone to or who he was with. Perhaps she wouldn't have liked it.

Miriam couldn't believe he was to be found walking around London streets. To her he seemed unimaginably far away, which was bad for her, but good when she thought about the knife. But then, just as her mother had predicted – like a miracle of wishing come true – he'd appeared on the street. Suddenly, there he was, and Miriam's heart had leapt with pleasure for a second at the sight of him, just from seeing his face, before she realized what was going to happen next. She hadn't seen her father for a year, but it took only an instant for her mother to make him turn and run away. Miriam had almost smiled at the sight of him, and her muscles tensed to run towards him, but it was all over in that fraction of a moment when their eyes locked. Or Miriam had thought they'd locked. Now, her mother would kill him. She would stick her knife in him. Miriam wasn't sure, apart from her mother swinging at nine o'clock one morning, what would happen after that.

Leah emerged, knifeless, from the gaping mouth of the underground about ten minutes later, her hair awry, face blackened by running mascara, muttering wildly to herself. Ray had managed to run faster than her and jump on a fortuitously waiting train. The station manager caught her, took the knife and had a sharp word or two. Then he let her go, seeing that she was more an emotionally distressed embarrassment than a public danger. Miriam and her mother walked home, while Leah described distractedly to her daughter and any interested passer-by exactly what she would have done to her bastard of a husband if she had only got near enough to him.

Miriam had said nothing, but from then on, whenever they were out, she kept a sharp eye open for any sign of her father, with the intention of distracting her mother until he got away unseen. But this time, looking all around Trafalgar Square from her rooted position outside South Africa House, she couldn't see him anywhere, and she knew he couldn't possibly be in a church. So why had her mother gone in there?

Miriam knew, though it had nothing much to do with religion, that she was a Jew. Like Alma Cogan, Frankie Vaughan and Jack Solomon. When they, or other Jews of note, were seen or heard of in newspapers or on television, that's what was said: '*He/She's Jewish.*' Like they were relatives. There was a special closeness and familiarity about these famous people, as if they were long lost cousins. Though they were from a richer or more talented branch of the family, their fame, nonetheless, was something to participate in. There wasn't any attention paid to religious observance – Passover passed them by and Friday evenings were just the beginning of the weekend – but to be Jewish was to be different. At Miriam's primary school, the kids would corner her in the playground and ask where she'd come from.

'I'm English.'

'No, you're not. You're a Jew. You come from Jewland.'

'I'm from Camden Town, England,' she'd say.

But they'd correct her, 'You can't be English, you're a Jew.'

Though Miriam was firm about her Englishness (once she brought her birth certificate into school), she knew they had a point. There was a difference. Though her family was no richer or better educated than the families of her friends at the local primary school, their houses smelled different, they ate different food, even spoke, indefinably, in a different way. Later, when the notion of class entered her consciousness, she tried to define her own, but found it hard to make an exact fit with any of the categories. They weren't middle-class professionals – her father was a travelling salesman, the only books in the house were children's books – but working class didn't work either. Lower middle class was approximate, though it wasn't right. Something from before, when neither she nor her parents were born, clung on and made the fit inexact. Sometimes middle-aged men with a glint in their eyes would stop her mother when she was out in the street with Miriam, and ask if she 'and her sister' were Italian. In those days in London, to have dark hair and eyes was to be foreign.

After Miriam's father vanished from their lives, Leah collapsed and spent most of her days lamenting: 'Help me, God. Help me, help me, God.' Though sometimes it was, 'Mummy, Mummy, help me, Mummy. Why did you have to die . . .' Alongside Miriam's anxiety at what her mother's incapacity meant for her own life, she developed a loathing of the sentimental despair of the distracted, disappointed woman who was unable to help

40

herself, but at least the God and the long-dead Mummy she wailed at were both Jewish, and somewhat familiar to Miriam as types. The God inside St Martin's-in-the-Fields was an alien being. A *goy*. He was supernatural, spooky, and utterly strange to Miriam. He hung limply with his eyes rolled heavenwards on a wooden cross, and blood trickled from various parts of his body. How could he help anyone when he couldn't help himself? People kissed his bloodied parts and wore him miniaturized round their necks, muttering incantations to him while their fingers fidgeted at beaded necklaces. Now Miriam's mother had entered this hopeless, helpless and creepy God's dark, dank, incense-smelling space. That her mother had turned to him in despair, and away from what seemed like the last familiar threads of her daughter's life, made Miriam feel, as she stood disconsolately outside South Africa House, that she was finally and utterly deserted.

When Leah emerged from the church after half an hour or so, she appeared unaltered, but to Miriam she had become detached. Even the demented woman with a knife was at least the mother she had known. This church-going woman was beyond Miriam's experience. They made their way back to their flat in silence. Neither of them ever mentioned Leah's detour into the land of the Father, Son and Holy Ghost, but Miriam, growing up fast if lopsidedly, felt it was a land of desperation; of helpless wishes, superstition and an attachment to fairy tales whose endings bore no relation to real life. For a while, her Jewishness became a small island, a patch of terra firma on which Miriam felt she could stand without sinking. It was not so much a religion as a geography for survival in an unaccountably fluid world.

When Ray left Leah and Miriam, Leah lost everything and Miriam watched as her mother's inner and outer life crumbled as if it had been built entirely of dreamstuff. She had heard her father complain that Leah had no interests beyond the home. But what, her mother retorted, did he expect of her? What was she supposed to be interested in? She made the home, he made the money; what else was there? For Ray there was another woman – younger, brighter, and more exciting – and a new life. For Leah, there was nothing. In Miriam's alarmed presence she wailed and wept and pledged revenge on the man who had taken all her hopes and what had become assumptions off with him. He had finally turned his back and gone. Not even the child held him in his unwanted home. They never heard from him again, or saw him apart from the fearful encounter in the Charing Cross Road.

The welfare system was in place by then, of course, but Leah's panic was too great for any kind of practicality. She imagined workhouses and soup kitchens, those real dangers she had grown up with, but worse to her was the idea of finding an official address and then getting forms, filling them in and then having to confess to a total stranger that after all her dreams she was as poor and without prospects as she had been in Brick Lane. That was too shameful to contemplate.

For a while a young rabbi had turned up and made himself useful, even raised her hopes for the future, but he, too, had deserted thanks, Leah told her daughter, to Miriam's sullenness. Leah was mystified by her life. How could it have come to this, returned to everything she had escaped from? Being once again poor and alone in the world, with the addition of a child to take care of, was so shattering, so improbable, so *inconceivable* that she had no idea what was to be done about it. She could keep a house nice, and look after Miriam, but only if she had the support a woman who could do nothing else needed. Suddenly her life had disintegrated, inexplicably. She was back where she started. Worse. She was back where she started and alone, without friends or family, as she had left the latter far behind and the former turned out to be Ray's friends rather than hers, disappearing as soon as he did.

Apart from the moment when she saw Ray in the street and chased him with her knife, she had no opportunity for revenge. Just after he left she went to his office and threw a brick through the window, but it turned out he had leased it to another company and gone away. She might have gone to jail but for the man who now owned the lease taking pity on her. He gave her a few pounds when he saw the state she was in and told her the insurance would take care of the windows. So she took to sitting in an armchair and weeping helpless rage into a once-ornamental handkerchief while calling on the God of the Hebrews and her dear, dead mother to come to her aid. And when no answer came, she tried her luck with the God of the Gentiles in Trafalgar Square. When that proved fruitless she gave up petitioning altogether and simply wailed, rocking briskly like someone in a hurry, wild-eyed in her chair.

One morning, after a particularly noisy night of lamentation, Miriam woke up to silence. The armchair her mother had taken to rocking in was empty, the tattered handkerchief abandoned on the seat. Leah was nowhere to be found. There was no message. Miriam went to school and when she returned home, the flat was as she had left it. Miriam wandered through the rooms, checking drawers and cupboards, looking for clues, but nothing was missing beyond her coat and handbag. There was no sign of her mother.

Nor was there ever again as far as Miriam was concerned. Leah slid out of her daughter's life (for all Miriam knew, out of life itself) with the same absence of explanation with which she had disappeared into the dark doorway of St Martin's-in-the-Fields. But this time she stayed in the dark. It was, Miriam knew, an unusual situation. Not one she had heard of before. She was not inclined to call the police, or mention her mother's absence to anyone at school, because she feared her mother might at any moment walk in the door and become hysterical with rage that Miriam had told other people about their private business. Miriam remained curiously calm about the vanishing, as if the earlier disappearance into the church had been practice for this event. *Then* she had been alarmed, disturbed and fearful for her future. It seemed to be that the present loss of her mother was only confirmation of what had already happened and to which Miriam had already had an appropriate reaction. She had felt desperately alone, utterly abandoned, standing outside South Africa House and watching her mother walk away from her and, for deeper reasons of trauma or helplessness perhaps, there was now no greater degree of aloneness she could feel, for all the apparent permanence of her mother's disappearance. It's possible that there is only a single experience of isolation in any one life, to which later events may refer, but not supersede. Perhaps it was as well to get it over and done with as soon as possible.

Miriam never saw or heard from her mother again. It didn't take long for the school to realize that Miriam was living on her own, and they alerted the social services, but despite their best efforts and those of the police, Leah apparently vanished without trace. Miriam began a new and uneventful life in the care of decent and affectionate foster parents where she slipped into the ordinary life of a child with the ease of an accomplished actor. At first she asked if anyone had heard of her mother, though with a politeness which suggested she felt it was expected of her. She lived another life in another place with people who were kind to her. She settled in remarkably well, everyone thought, including Miriam, who allowed her mother's disappearance to be something that had happened, not something that continued. She did not think of Leah very often – there was nothing very much to think about her.

As the sensible doctor predicted, her childish nightmares had eventually come to an end. Apparently she stopped being afraid of growing up, or, at least, realized there was nothing she could do about it. But it was as if the price was that she had to stop dreaming entirely. She had never recalled having a dream, bad or good, since. Very occasionally, something would jog what felt like a memory of a place in which, when she thought about it, she'd never been, or a person she'd never known. Apart from those faint flashes of place or identity, she never got any kind of narrative back from her dreaming just as she hadn't from the nightmares. She supposed she did dream, knowing that everyone did, and sometimes wished she could remember hers vividly, as other people could. Often when she woke she mentally quizzed herself, hoping to find some story she had told herself while she slept, but there never was anything more than a rare, half-grasped *déjà vu* which bore no resemblance to her real life.

44

But although she sometimes strove for her dream memory, she was also aware that the lack of it might be to her advantage. What if the nightmares hadn't in fact stopped and her mind had simply learned to deal with them by blanking them out? For all she knew, that was true. For all she knew, she might spend every night in torment, but as long as the horror evaporated on waking and she remained ignorant, she could not be bothered by it. Realizing this, she didn't push herself too far to retrieve her dreams.

Sleep, since the nightmares had stopped disturbing Mimi's nights, was just rest, an absence of waking consciousness pure and simple, or so it had seemed for much of her life. Only lately had it come to be anything more, or as Jack put it, pathological. She had never had much trouble getting to sleep, but now, in the past few weeks, she had the greatest difficulty staying awake. Just this week, apart from dropping off tonight during the movie, she had fallen asleep in the middle of a dinner party Jack had organized for a business contact, and just after breakfast while discussing Jack's summer holiday plans.

It was as if a veil of water-sodden grey mist came down over her, between herself and the world, and no matter what stimulation the world might be offering at the time, the pull of the mist was irresistible. The reality around her would recede like a star expanding away from the centre of the universe, becoming more and more distant, losing the volume and clarity of an item of the world, and however hard she tried to follow its retreat the mist always prevented her from keeping up. Within seconds she was asleep, although from her point of view the next thing that happened was that she woke up and found Jack looking poisonously at her – because the only common element in the circumstances of this public sleeping was that Jack was always present.

The first couple of times it happened Jack had been amused. It was a conceit of his to enjoy subverting well-mannered social occasions with a visible contempt for the polite banalities people settled for when they got together socially. Initially, he saw

45

Mimi's capacity for public sleep in the same light, applauding her on the way home for causing bafflement and embarrassment among the genteelensia. It seemed he thought she had become an activist (through the clever paradox of inaction) in his campaign. But soon Mimi was falling sleep when just the two of them were together and there was no third party for whom he could imagine she was expressing their shared disdain. His irritation began to grow as it dawned on him that her sleep was an avoidance of him rather than a statement of social defiance.

All Mimi knew was that she fell asleep a lot. She also knew that she was unhappy with Jack, but she chose not to put those two pieces of information too closely together.

'Maybe I'm ill,' she said.

'I was in the middle of *talking* to you,' Jack fumed, after shaking her awake. 'How the fuck could you fall asleep?'

'I must have been tired,' was her initial effort.

Jack exploded.

'Don't be fucking stupid. You slept like a log last night, and even if they're tired people don't fall dead asleep in the middle of a conversation.'

That was when she suggested she could be ill, though she could have answered instead that they had not in fact been in the middle of a conversation when she'd fallen asleep, but that Jack had been telling her a string of implausible and insulting lies.

'Then go to the fucking doctor,' Jack shouted and luckily left the room because Mimi could feel the grey mist beginning to descend.

'What are you thinking?' her doctor asked.

'Catalepsy?' she offered, feeling idiotic.

The doctor shook his head with a slight smile, offering her another go.

'Brain tumour? Don't you . . . fall asleep?'

'Yes, it can be a symptom. Have you had any headaches?' Mimi shook her head. 'How are things going in your life at the moment?'

'OK. Things are OK,' Mimi said, closing down that avenue of enquiry.

'Well, we'll have a brain scan done, just to put your mind at rest.' He smiled faintly at the faint pun. 'But I think it's extremely unlikely there's anything organically wrong. When we get the results, come back and we'll see if we can find out a bit more about what's going on with you.'

Mimi didn't bother to confirm the offered appointment for the brain scan. She didn't go back to her GP. There was no need to, she knew why she was falling asleep.

But even though she knew that the mind had the capacity to dominate the soma, she still found it hard to credit her mental self with such practical power over her physical body. Yes, if you were mentally low the chances were you'd catch a cold. Yes, if you were anxious about an exam your heart might palpitate as if you'd run a fast mile. But to drop off to sleep in any and every circumstance because the need for escape was so great, seemed a trick too complex for even the most domineering of psyches. But once she let go of the comforting thought of life-threatening disease, it was clear what her behaviour was about, and there was hardly any point in denying that her psyche was working overtime. In any case, Mimi was not blind to her circumstances. She knew what there was to know about them.

Tonight, Jack had come in at an ordinary hour and said, 'Let's go to a movie.' He had not arrived home the previous three nights before four in the morning, but tonight it appeared he had nowhere to go, and rather than stay at home and face the possibility of the two of them spending the evening together alone, he had proposed the safety of the cinema: a dark, noise-filled public space which precluded speech and yet which had a semblance of normality about it. Didn't couples go to the movies together, wasn't it a perfectly natural thing to do in perfectly natural circumstances? It was an ideal protection for the continuation of the lie.

'Fine,' said Mimi, not bothering to ask what he'd thought of seeing.

They had not had an evening out together for weeks, or perhaps it was months now, but they set off, like a proper couple and walked to the local cinema where, it turned out, a stylish film about a quartet of friends in a love tangle, much recommended by the critics, was showing. Mimi had barely spoken on the way, letting Jack do all the talking – a run through of his busy day, deals he had half made, idiocies his partner had perpetrated which he had had to correct, the useless incompetence of people he was obliged to do business with. It was the usual fury that Jack accumulated during a day at work. The eventfulness of his days had always astounded Mimi, whose days were so very different, and the energy with which he spoke and strode along the street jarred against the accumulated silence of Mimi's day, wearying her step by step and rendering her incapable of making more than a few murmured sounds in response to his monologue. In any case, the more he talked the greater was the weight of what he was not saying. Mimi grew morose with resentment that she had allowed herself to go along with this evening out, which shouted normality and whispered something altogether different.

What she wanted to say was 'So she's busy this evening? Or maybe she just wants an evening to herself,' but against the certainty of his confidently told lie which would incorporate the fact that he didn't care whether she believed it or not, she held her tongue. The wittily scripted film was just ten minutes in before Mimi began to lose the thread of it, the voices grew distant and echoey, as if they were coming from another room, and she dropped off, beside her treacherous lover, into a dreamless and sullen unconsciousness.

What had happened after she woke was unusual. Mimi was surprised that she had walked away from Jack after the movie. She did not think of herself as one who leaves, but as one who was left. It seemed to her to be the more secure option. It was her habit, her decision, to experience the act of leaving from the point of view of those who stayed behind; to her, those who walked away rendered themselves invisible. More than that, for the one left behind, they dissolved out of being. Leavers relinquished their reality, were nullified and came to exist only in the dubious world of memory. Absence was a matter of perspective. Those who had walked away from Mimi made themselves absent to her, creating a hole where they had been in her life. They became only memories, pictures from a dead past. Those who stay behind continue, while those who go no longer have a narrative. When her father and then her mother left, their stories came to an abrupt end as they left Mimi's story. But she continued, and there was a comforting certainty in that. Mimi was appalled by the idea that those who walked away might still inhabit a life of their own, and she did not want to put this to the test by being one herself. As soon as she could leave her foster home, she got herself a place of her own and never went to live, or even spend the night, with other people. They came to her, at her insistence, and they left the next morning or months later, while she stayed where she was. There had been one-night stands, boyfriends, grand passions even, but all had been conducted on her territory, and all, when they were over, had left her where she was already. *They* became absent, *she* remained. Trivial though this evening's event was, she would not, had she stopped to think for a moment, have walked away from Jack in the cinema. It didn't matter though, because she was home again, Jack was absent, and now, with a little help from the Valium, the incident began to fade into the damp mist that came over her consciousness, and disappeared as reliably as her dreams. Soon, Mimi was asleep for the second time that evening secure in the knowledge that when she woke no dream memories would disturb her day.

Jack had made light work of her carefully constructed wall of serenity. It turned out to be fatally flawed. Good enough to keep most of the world at a distance, but of little use against someone as hungry and angry as Jack, who saw a wall and wanted whatever was behind it, simply because it was there and hidden, simply because it was valued by someone. Mimi had not reckoned that her wall might be breached merely by Jack blasting it alternately with lust and appreciation. His fervent conviction that serenity shared would be serenity doubled seeped into her, until it seemed not just reasonable, but positively desirable. If her silence was real and valuable, it could not be damaged by sharing it with someone else who wanted the same thing as her. The idea was new and alluring. She fell in love with it as much as with Jack. Both loves, along with the vivid sex they contrived together, served to blanket any more realistic observations of Jack.

Mimi didn't know exactly when – what day, which moment – the lying had started. She had known from very early on in her relationship with Jack that she wouldn't be able to tell when it began, that she could be certain only that it would. Knowing the lying would start, she was left with just the hope that she would catch the lies as they came. It was a small hope. In the event, her own intense, self-protecting suspicion made it all the more difficult to tell when reality had taken over from her paranoia. She watched out for them from the beginning, assuming every day that now they had begun, but knowing also (and with subtle self-deception) that she needed to believe he had lied already in order to protect herself from being deluded when it actually came. She had known since their first adulterous trip to Paris that with Jack she was up against a liar of the first quality. She also knew from long-ago experience that paranoia was never to be taken lightly. Not when it came to that tingling sense of distrust about what people were really up to in their relations with her.

Three years before their miserable outing to the cinema, Tricia had been Jack's wife and Mimi his bright, shiny, new lover. Jack had to make a business trip to Paris in pursuit of finance for his latest venture, the most recent project that no one else had thought of, another glaring consumer gap just waiting to be filled – Jack's speciality. This time, he planned to produce popular road maps of Europe, brightly and wittily illustrated, showing what people really wanted to see: how to get to famous places, vineyards, spas, museums, out-of-the-way hotels and the best beaches. They'd be jokey and amusing, showing only the routes – and cunning short cuts – to where people on holiday wanted to go, and best of all, Jack reckoned, it was an ideal project for sponsorship. The Perrier Guide to Watering Holes. The Mouton-Rothschild Guide to Great Grape Country. The Raleigh Guide to the Steepest Mountain Roads in Europe.

However, the maps were not the only glaring gap which a trip to Paris would begin to fill. Mimi had known Jack for three months. They were in a cyclone of passion that was fed by insufficiency. Earning her living as a dressmaker and living alone had proved convenient at the beginning of her affair with Jack. Clients came by appointment, she worked in her own time, and her flat was her own and therefore available to suit Jack's married schedule. Sometimes Jack dropped in first thing in the morning for sex, once or twice a week he took a foodless lunch with her, and every evening she was free to fit in with his plans. In fact, they saw a great deal of each other, once the early reticence of once a week had escalated into fervour. Mimi's elastic schedule made their increasing passion easy – only Jack's commitments limited their opportunities.

He came to her each evening, early, during that time when he would normally be having an after-work drink with colleagues. Mimi and Jack made love, lay together for a while and then Jack had to go home. They had never spent an entire night waking, sleeping, loving in each other's arms. The idea of a whole night together tantalized them. The limitation of a few hours after which they were obliged to let each other go made the idea of a full night unachievably desirable. They had never had enough of each other by the time Jack had to go back to Tricia, but even a stolen, irresistible extra hour of love-making – a risk to Jack's marriage that neither of them wanted – didn't satisfy. More only made them want more. It began to look to them as if they wanted more than more time simply for more sex. They hankered also for time simply to lie together, to see the dawn break in the sweaty acrid air they had created, fetid and deliciously the mingling of their own secretions given independent life. They longed to experience waking from the shores of desire-disturbed sleep with the other still next to them, available, and to reach out, barely conscious yet but hungrily to start again. And again. One dawn didn't seem enough. Nights and days and nights, a marathon of naked togetherness was what they wanted, achingly. And, at last, like a reward for their three months' forbearance, days and nights (with the occasional business lunch interrupting) was what Paris was going to give them.

As much as anything the illustrated map idea was borne out of Jack's need for unlimited time with Mimi. At that point, a brilliant fortune-netting idea which required him to spend a lot of time at home researching it would have been put on the back burner. This brilliant new plan was fertilized by sexual desire and the necessity to find a good reason to get away from home for an extended period. His first mapping plans – or, more accurately, sexual fantasies – revolved around the Caribbean, South America, Africa, the Indian Ocean, but Jack was realistic enough to give up the exotic beaches of Brazil in favour, at least initially, of a more explicable trip to Paris. However, he kept Tobago, Brazil, and Mauritius in mind for the future. The expansion of his commercial horizons and the application of glistening suntan lotion to the sweating crevices of Mimi's body were to be the happy co-consequences of business success. Jack was not one to settle for a single reason for doing anything he wanted to do. His reasonings expanded into bouquets of multi-specied justifications. Just inventing a non-existent business trip to get his hands on Mimi's nights wouldn't have done. And the prospect of a deal was not enough on its own to have given the trip a real piquancy. Jack was a motivational capitalist, a promiscuous rationalizer. He wanted everything he could get in one package, if it was full to bursting, so much the better, and he wanted it – whatever it was, everything – right now.

The seat-belt light went off on the plane to Paris, and Mimi got up to have a pee before the drinks cart made it impossible to negotiate the aisle. She entered the stainless steel cubicle and made to push the folding door closed behind her, but met resistance as Jack slid into the tiny space with her, squeezing her against the toilet bowl to make enough room to shut the door.

'What are you doing?' she gasped, laughing at the crowd they made.

'Fucking you in an aeroplane toilet,' he said, unzipping his trousers. 'Brace yourself.'

'They'll see . . . they have smoke alarms . . . probably cameras . . .'

'So don't smoke, and say cheese when you come. Hitch up your skirt.'

She braced her forearms against the back wall and stood with her feet to either side of the toilet bowl, her face, resting on her hands, turned to the right, giving her a view of the two of them in the mirror above the washbasin. It was, as it turned out, a perfect sexual space, confining their movement, defining and refining their degree of closeness. Jack pressed himself hard against Mimi's back and buttocks, supporting himself with one hand on the back wall, the other around her torso, and entered her from behind. Mimi watched his thighs flexing in the mirror as he pushed himself deeper into her, and her own hips answering with a rhythmic backward thrust to get him deeper into her still. They celebrated the start of their first entire week together with a mutual orgasm in a toilet high in the sky. She took his hand from her ribcage and pressed it against her mouth, partly to stop any sound escaping from her (in case they had a microphone in there as well) and also to suck on the flesh of his palm, to taste him and feel him against her teeth and tongue. They came with his head buried in her shoulder and hers flung back, rubbing the side of her face against his coarse curls. He hissed when he came, as if a 'yes' had taken him over and squeezed the breath from his lungs.

Jack slid his tongue deep into her mouth while she finally had her pee and then they straightened each other's clothes before opening the door.

'Will you piss on me when we're in Paris?' he asked her.

She'd never urinated on anyone before, but she thought she might.

Jack left first, and Mimi followed, their faces each a picture of excessive innocence, as the woman who was waiting to use the lavatory next stepped back to allow the unexpected second occupant to make her exit. As soon as they were back in their seats a stewardess arrived with a bottle of champagne.

'Newly-weds?' she asked, dead-pan.

Jack and Mimi merely stared at her.

'We always give newly-weds a complimentary bottle of champagne,' she said, with just the merest hint of amusement. She held the bottle out and Jack reached for it with an ingenuous smile.

'You *are* married, aren't you?' she checked, withdrawing the bottle slightly from Jack's grasp.

Jack and Mimi nodded vigorously, telling only half a lie; one of them was.

'To each other?' the stewardess queried, knowing all the right questions.

Jack and Mimi tried to laugh in the way they thought innocent newly-weds might, and failed, but got the bottle nevertheless.

'See,' Mimi whispered when she'd gone. 'They had a camera in there.'

'Lucky them,' said Jack. 'I'd like to see that movie. Anyway, we're better than newly-weds. Without us fucking the world would stop going round.'

Mimi didn't believe it, but she didn't say so. She allowed herself the possibility of thinking it might be so, at the beginning of their trip which was to give them six whole nights together alone with each other.

The days and nights hazed together. Jack had arranged it so that he didn't have a business meeting until Wednesday lunch-time. Monday and Tuesday were spent in each other's arms. Sex slid into light, hallucinated sleep and out again, back to their bodies, which when even half awake craved for more of the more they were having more of. Hunger forced them out for meals, walking close, keeping physical contact, as if, separated, they might collapse, their muscles and bones too fluid with use to keep them upright. They ate slowly and sipped wine until, their stomachs satisfied, the other craving returned, and skipping coffee they headed like sleep-walkers back to the centre of their lives, their hotel room, their double bed.

Jack sipped from his wine glass on the bedside table and dropped his mouth to Mimi's breast, swilling the wine around her nipple before swallowing. When he let wine fall from his mouth into her open mouth, she urged, 'More, more.' He worked his saliva into a white froth on his lips, showing it to her before letting it drop, and receiving it, she shivered again, 'More, more.' She wanted more of everything, and returned his gifts with enthusiasm. She dipped a finger into her wet cunt and ran it across Jack's mouth while he whispered, 'More, more.' She pushed several fingers deep into herself and let him suck on them hard and noisily. They encouraged every sign of greed in each other, whipping up their appetite, and giving in to any whim and fancy.

'Do you know,' Jack said while they rested against one another, 'you are exactly what I imagined when I was an adolescent. I lay in bed on Saturday mornings, masturbating, trying to think up the woman of my dreams. What you are, what you do, your hunger, your greed, your shamelessness are exactly what I invented. She was you. I've never met her before. You belong to me. We belong to each other.'

This was considerably further than either of them had intended to go at the beginning of their affair. Or so Mimi thought. She heard him and stayed quiet, putting his words firmly out of her mind both for what they meant, and what they meant to her. Part of the thrill of what they were doing was the danger, the way they had stepped right up to some line that each of them had firmly assured the other was not to be overstepped. Now they were dancing along on it, light-headed, like drunken tightrope walkers, and getting to the other side was not their central aim.

On Wednesday morning, anguished that at last they would have to separate for a couple of hours, they clung to each other after making love for the last time before he had to leave, as if it were the last time of all. Jack lay above Mimi, stroking her hair and planting small kisses around her face and neck.

'Oh, dear,' he sighed, serious and doomed.

'What?'

'This wasn't supposed to happen.'

She might have let it go, but she couldn't stop herself asking for the words.

'What?'

'This. What's happened between us. I've never felt so close to anyone, felt anyone so close to me. It was just going to be an affair.' There was something almost despairing in his voice.

She might have resisted and answered, 'It is.' The words were there, ready to be used. It was a moment when she could have re-directed their route into what it had been intended to be: an aimless journey, though later she doubted if that was ever Jack's real inclination.

'I know,' she whispered, holding him tighter in her arms, and floated along on the tide.

'I love you,' said Jack, momentously, with a sob in his voice.

'I love you,' Mimi said after a pause, allowing herself to feel that the undertow was a force outside themselves and too strong to be denied.

That evening, as Mimi was dressing for the first time that day to go out to dinner, Jack phoned his wife.

'Otherwise, she'll phone me.'

Mimi took herself off to the bathroom and, watching herself naked in the mirror, began brushing her teeth. She didn't shut the door – they no longer shut doors on each other – nakedness was the norm, and what they did to their own bodies was as available for the pleasure of the observing lover as what they did to each other. She tried not to listen to Jack on the phone, but she picked up his tone which was friendly and informative. He'd done this, seen that, set up meetings, may have got a bite from the Perrier people. Then, after a pause, the tone changed. His voice dropped into a fierce insistence.

'Don't be *silly*! Of course not.'

A pause and then anger and furious impatience. The sound of someone outraged and insulted by false accusation, but also of someone dealing with a child beyond reason who needed firmness and reassurance to bring them back to reality. Mimi listened, deliberately now, toothbrush idle inside her mouth foaming with paste.

'No! I said *no!* I don't lie, you know that. You've got to stop this. You're being crazy. There's no one. *No one.* I'm alone. I have been and I will be until I see you on Sunday. Now, stop it. All right? I said, all right? That's my girl. And no more silliness . . .'

Another pause.

'Good. All right. I'll speak to you tomorrow. 'Bye.'

It was not Jack's words but the conviction behind them that made Mimi wonder if she was actually standing naked, his semen dripping down her thighs, toothbrush in hand, in his hotel room in Paris while the phone call was going on. It didn't seem likely. He had almost persuaded her, an eavesdropper, of her own impossibility. She didn't know if Tricia really believed him, but Mimi was as good as certain that Jack was not sleeping with anyone while he was away on his business trip.

In a moment Jack walked in to the bathroom. Mimi began to move the toothbrush across her teeth slowly, looking at Jack in the mirror.

'OK, that's done. Come on, I'm starving. You're still not dressed.' Then he groaned. 'Oh, God, here we go again,' and pressed his stiffening erection up against her buttocks. 'Dinner can wait a few more minutes. I want to fuck you with your mouth full of toothpaste.'

If Mimi was a little distant during that bathroom encounter, Jack didn't seem to notice. He enjoyed the changes in her: loved her ability to take control and make demands, but also the way, sometimes, she was passive and receiving. Mimi didn't just go through the motions. By then her body was so highly charged that the slightest touch from Jack set her nerves thrumming towards a climax. She moaned as he caressed her and cried out as he lifted her on to the washbasin and entered her. 'I love you,' she sobbed for the second time, as she came, but there was a part of her that remained separate, still blinking, as it were, her astonishment at Jack's assured performance on the phone to his wife. There was even an aspect of it that increased her sexual excitement. The dissonance between his 'I don't lie, you know that' and the pressure of his rock-hard cock pounding at her cervix was breathtaking. The same voicebox that spoke into the telephone receiver, though not the same voice, called out to her that he loved her – also for the second time – as he came.

'I love you . . . God, I love you.'

And while he came, while she felt her own body throbbing with pleasure, she wondered if Tricia back in London was now feeling relieved of her anxieties about what her husband might be up to. Had Jack made Tricia feel better and then come into the bathroom to make Mimi feel better?

But ever since then, Mimi had no doubts that the lying would start for her, too, and that she might only be able to tell he was lying by a special quality of absolute conviction in his voice when he denied it.

On the night flight home, there was a thick silence between them that spoke of separation, of returning to their old intermittent meetings. Mimi wondered if it wouldn't have been better not to have had these days and nights, if going back to what they had before wouldn't now be worse. She felt him sliding away from her, preparing to meet Tricia, readjusting himself to a life she had no knowledge of at all. Every now and then their eyes would meet and allow a moment of recognition of the strain of parting. Mimi told herself she was being idiotic. This was already more than she had intended with him. How could they not return to their previous lives? She would meet Simon later in the week, they would have dinner and make love. It was necessary she should so that not too much was made of the trip to Paris. And Jack would return home to Tricia, to their routine, whatever it was, their familiarity. They would make love, he would give her the scent Mimi had refused to help him choose for her. It was right to return to normal. Still, the air was sullen and sad between them.

'Tell me a story,' she said, turning to Jack with a smile,

trying to make the air clearer.

'I love you. That's a true story,' Jack said mournfully.

'No, a story. Go on, tell me.'

'I don't know any stories. You tell me one. Tell me something that happened to you when you were a kid.'

Mimi sipped her wine.

'Nothing happened. There isn't any story.'

But Jack could see she was thinking. She had something in mind.

'Go on,' Jack urged.

'It's not very nice.'

'Good.'

'Well, it was when I was living away from home. With a family I'd been sent to during a summer holiday to give my mother a break. I'd made some friends – local street kids, not respectable like the people I was staying with. We used to hang out, Jason and his brother and a couple of other kids, in a derelict house. The council had boarded it up but we got in round the back. One day, Jason turned up with this dog.'

'What dog?'

'A dog. A little dog. A smooth haired thing, about the size of a large cat. It was brownish, with big, soppy doggy eyes. He said it had followed him, so he put his belt round its neck and brought it to our meeting place. There was just me and Jason, who was a bit older than me, and Derek, his younger brother. Jason said he couldn't take it home, because his mum wouldn't have animals in the house. And, of course, I couldn't take it, because I wasn't living at home. I said, "What are we going to do with it, then?" Because it was as if we were responsible for it. If a dog follows you and you ignore it, that's one thing. But if you put a belt round its neck, and take it with you, then it's yours. You're lumbered. I didn't mind dogs. I didn't like them especially, but I didn't mind them.' Mimi shrugged her neutrality.

'So? Did you keep it?'

Mimi shook her head and taking Jack's hand, dipped his finger into her glass and sucked the wine off it, thoughtfully.

'Not exactly. We did and we didn't.'

'What does that mean?'

'We ate it.'

Jack remained silent for a moment. Mimi let the silence continue.

'Why didn't you just let it go?' he asked eventually.

'That's what Jason suggested. But I didn't think it was right. As I said, we'd taken it on, and it seemed to like us. It went racing round, yapping like mad, and jumping on us, wagging its tail so much I thought it'd break. Eventually, it took a flying leap at me, and ended up in my arms. It went all floppy, and just lay there looking up at me, sort of blissful. It was heart-rending, I don't mind telling you. That's when I suggested we eat it.'

'*You* suggested eating it?'

'Yes.'

'Why?'

Mimi shrugged.

'It seemed like the right thing to do. I liked the little creature. I didn't want to leave it wandering around, it might have got run over or something. It seemed a good idea. It just came to me.'

'Yes, I see,' Jack said solemnly.

'So there was a bit of a discussion. Jason didn't think we should, and his brother – well, he was a bit thick and didn't have much of an idea of what he thought about anything. But funnily enough, he was the one who clinched it. He said, "I've never eaten a dog." Jason and I collapsed laughing, and the dog seemed to enjoy the joke, too. He jumped out of my arms and belted round and round, barking like it was the funniest things he'd ever heard. When we calmed down a bit, we agreed that none of us had eaten dog, but Jason had heard that the Japanese or someone, did, and we fell to wondering what it tasted like. And there it was.'

Laughter lodged in Jack's throat broke through.

'You're a monster. What a terrible thing to do,' Jack hiccuped, trying to control himself.

'I told you it wasn't going to be a very nice story.'

'So who killed the poor little bugger?'

'We decided to do it together. All of us. Oh, and we gave it a name, too. We baptized it for the sake of its soul, Jason and his brother being practising Catholics. We called it . . .'

'Fido!' Jack pre-empted.

'Fang, as a matter of fact,' Mimi said with dignity. 'Jason had been doing the Aztecs, or maybe it was the Incas, at school. Whichever it was that did ritual killings. So we got a slab of concrete from the garden, and laid Fang out on it. He seemed quite happy, and stayed there while I said some mumbo-jumbo that was supposed to be an Aztec incantation, and then, on the count of three, we laid into him with our penknives, all at the same time.'

'That's awful,' Jack wailed, mourning Fang's fate even as another bubble of laughter rose in his gullet. Mimi, however, got serious.

'It was the only warm thing I'd ever killed,' she said quietly, as if she were speaking to herself or in the confessional.

'What?' Jack asked, the bubble vanishing.

'I'd killed things before – insects, worms, you know, the way kids do. But that was the first time I killed something warm to the touch. Something that, you know, really felt alive. And when he was dead, I lifted him up – offering him up to the gods, as it were . . . He was so limp. I've never felt anything as *loose* as that, yet warm still. Anyway,' she said, coming back to the story and turning to look at Jack. 'Then we cooked him. Roasted him on an open fire in the garden. Proper little boy scouts, we were.'

'And?'

'And what?'

'Did you eat him?'

'Of course we did. But very respectfully, like Aztecs eating the heart of their enemy. Only we didn't eat the inside bits, just a leg each because we got a bit queasy when we cut him open and saw what the inside looked like. It didn't taste bad at all, though. And then we buried the remains of Fang, with full military honours, like a fallen comrade, in the overgrown flowerbed.'

'Were you ever sorry?'

61

'About Fang? I felt sorry now and then when I'd see a kid in the street with a dog, and I'd remember Fang. He'd have been one of those devoted dogs. But as soon as I thought that, I was glad we'd killed him.'

'Why?'

Mimi shook her head. 'I don't know. I was just glad. Who wants a dog dragging round after you all the time?'

Jack stared at her with a question doggy-paddling in his single limpid blue eye. Beneath the surface, Mimi could see the distorted shape of desire coming up for air.

'You're right,' he said, keeping his eye steady. 'Best to eat them.' He reached for her under the airplane blanket they had spread for warmth over their knees.

Even with the best will in the world and the help of the Valium, Mimi's sleep that night after she returned alone from the cinema did not go undisturbed. Jack got home sometime after one. After vomiting noisily into the toilet bowl he crawled into bed where Mimi lay curled up, ostensibly asleep, with her back turned against Jack's side of the bed. He lifted the duvet and saw she was wearing a T-shirt and knickers.

'Bitch,' he said, and inserted a flat hand between the backs of her thighs, fumbling to reach inside the elasticized gusset of her knickers. He bent over her and whispered in her ear while he wriggled two fingers into the moist place between her legs and began a rhythmic stroking of her clitoris. 'Have you been waiting for me? You have been waiting for me, haven't you?'

His voice took on a nudging insistence to match the practised urging of his finger. Both were intended to induce in his apparently sleeping bedfellow a shift into a waking compliance with something known and well rehearsed between them.

'Come on,' he incited. 'You've been waiting for me. Come on.'

Mimi's thighs relaxed their resistance against his intrusion as she felt the power of his seductive voice and touch mix dangerously and excitingly with the coldness and dislike that had come from him in the cinema. She knew, of course, that hers was the second clitoris to have been stroked towards desire by his fingers that night. She could smell the other one as Jack's spare hand pushed the hair away from her face. The alien but familiar scent on his fingers, and the fact that Jack had not bothered to wash it off only sharpened Mimi's appetite for their story. Once, the empty sexual game they sometimes played, fast, hungry with an undertone of violation, had stoked their desire for each other, seeming to tell secrets about their other natures while taking away their specificity and drawing them into a delicious and passionate anonymity. Now that anonymous otherness of the smell on his fingers, the contemptuous insult of it, added something acrid, arid even, but not less exciting.

Mimi shifted a little, more nearly over on to her back and she drew in a long breath that signified something other than the disturbance of her sleep. They drew together, close and fierce, and she began to whisper into his ear, her voice low, almost a monotone. 'Fuck you, fuck you, I don't want you.' He spread her legs apart with the palms of his hands and slipped inside her, moving slowly and carefully so as not to disturb the monologue.

When it was finished she pulled away from him and turned over on her side.

'Back to sleep, Princess?' Jack muttered dangerously in the darkness.

'It's my new life's work. I don't want you here any more,' she said in a voice quite different from the one she had used during their sexual encounter.

As if her answer was the final, insupportable round in the battle between them, Jack slid speechlessly out of bed, put his clothes back on, collected together his suits and his word processor, threw his key on the kitchen table, and left the flat. Mimi lay in bed watching Jack's things being carried out, as she had watched them being carried in two years before: without comment.

Mimi continued to lie in bed, staring at the empty space Jack had left behind him, and considered her position. Jack had left her for good, there was no doubt, but then Jack was always going to leave her at some point, and the fact that it had come was no more than the future arriving much as it had been expected to arrive. Now, rather than later; but it always turned out to be now, the future, when it came. Not having Jack living with her would alter the circumstances of her life, she supposed, after he had closed the door behind him none too quietly, but only in the sense that she would be living alone again and an episode had concluded and slipped into her past. It was an item of punctuation, but not the end of her story. As ever, she remained where she was and someone else had gone. Jack went to live in the same limbo territory as her absent mother. Wherever that was was no waking concern of Mimi's. She went back to sleep within minutes of Jack's final exit.

Bella

Bella sat on the wooden chair with her hands clasped together on her lap. Her head was bent down towards the bible which lay open on the small table in front of her. As her eyes read the text, her lips moved, though only the merest sibilance disturbed the stillness.

> *By the rivers of Babylon, there we sat down, yea, we*
> *wept, when we remembered Zion.*
> *We hanged our harps upon the willows in the midst*
> *thereof.*
> *For there they that carried us away captive required*
> *of us a song;*
> *And they that wasted us required of us mirth, saying,*
> *'Sing us one of the songs of Zion.'*
> *How shall we sing the Lord's song in a strange land?*
> *If I forget thee, O Jerusalem, let my right hand forget*
> *her cunning.*
> *If I do not remember thee, let my tongue cleave to the*
> *roof of my mouth . . .*

Her words, barely audible in the small, bleak room, trailed off into silence.

A great fear filled her as the immensity of her loneliness overflowed her available vacant internal spaces. She put up a bit of a fight. God knew her, she consoled herself, but the thought meant nothing to her. Nothing that could protect her against her fear. Which meant that no one knew her, no one in this world, and there was no other. The fear returned, in all its arctic emptiness.

But hadn't she dedicated herself to the idea of living *as if* there

65

was a God? And consequently, wasn't it *as if* God knew and understood her, and she was therefore not alone after all? Yes, she was alone, *in reality*, but no more so than every single individual in the world, and like everyone else, she had a source of illusory comfort. If God was real he would have been beyond her comprehension, therefore illusion was necessity; illusion *was* faith, all the faith there could be. Wasn't that true? Had she not thought this through and made it her central truth?

She forced her eyes to focus again, to turn the blurred page of the bible back into a psalm, which she tried to continue. No sound came. Her lips moved, her throat strained, but there was no voice.

She turned the pages in a building panic. *Hear my prayer, O Lord, and let my cry come unto thee* . . . her eyes read, but her voice would not. *Make a joyful noise unto the Lord* . . . Nothing. *I will sing of mercy and judgement: unto thee, O Lord, will I sing* . . . But there was only silence.

Bella had a problem. It was not that she no longer believed in God, because she never had and she'd managed to find a way around the difficulty. It was that she no longer believed in *faith*, and it seemed that reasoning could no longer find a way around that.

There was a knock on the door. Bella got up and opened it.

Mel from downstairs stood there in her slippers with her toddler on her hip. His nose was running, and his eyes were watery.

'Hi. Sorry to bother you, but my fucking meter's run out and I haven't got a bean till my giro comes through. I don't know what the fuck's holding it up. The bastards said it'd be here by today. He's got a cold and it's freezing down there.' Mel nodded to the little boy, who started to cough on cue, but genuinely. She jiggled him a bit, but he went on coughing. 'Oh, shit, he's off again. You haven't got a few quid to spare, have you? Just till my giro arrives?'

Bella opened her mouth as if to say something, then closed it and just nodded. She went to a small bowl on the mantelpiece above the gas fire and took out the five-pound note which was all there was in it, apart from a folded giro-cheque. She handed the money silently to Mel who took it with a grateful smile.

'Oh, ta. You haven't got any coins? It's all right, I'll nip out to the shop and get it changed.' She turned to go back downstairs but stopped and looked at the other woman still standing in the doorway. 'You all right? Not talking today?' She looked past Bella into the room. 'It's as cold up here as downstairs. Your fire's not on.' She looked down at the five-pound note in her hand for a moment. 'Are you sure you can spare this? You don't need . . .?'

Bella made a quick smile and shook her head insistently, pushing Mel's offering palm closed over the money. Mel looked relieved.

'Well, if you're sure?' she said, and made for the stairs as the little boy's cough grew louder and chestier. 'I'd better go and get him warmed up. Thanks, Leah.'

Bella returned to her straight-backed chair and pulled her old woollen cardigan tightly around her, securing it with her folded arms. It was an unconscious gesture intended to do more than increase warmth, though it was icy cold in the room. She hadn't had the fire on since the previous morning. When the meter had run out she'd looked in the bowl for change but found only the five-pound note. It was all she had, apart from the giro-cheque that had come in the post the day before. She had looked at the note and the cheque for a while, and then taken her cardigan from the wardrobe and put it on over her dress and jumper, preferring the cold to the idea of knocking on anyone's door to ask for change, or having to go out to the post office two streets away. She'd slept in her clothes last night and when the morning came, as it did for her at dawn every day, she'd seemed to have adjusted to the temperature a bit. It wasn't unbearable, she thought, not as unbearable as the prospect of going out. She told herself that tomorrow would do for cashing the giro, though now she thought that if Mel's money came by tomorrow she could put off going out until the following day.

She had too much on her mind for going out, and even the briefest of encounters was distracting. Just that moment with Mel at the door had disturbed her, though she was a nice girl, doing her best to manage on her own with no man and no job and that little boy forever coughing and crying. Apart from her language, Mel always behaved decently when they occasionally met coming in or out of the house. But *why* did she have to call her Leah, like that? Of course, it wasn't her fault. Why wouldn't she, she didn't know any different? It was the name she'd given Mel when they'd met first on the stairs and Mel had asked. She'd started to give her name, but her mind went blank, and in the silence the old name just came out. It had made her head reel, saying it again. 'Leah.'

A couple of days later, at the post office, the man behind the counter had handed her giro money to her through the slot under the thief-proof glass with a friendly smile and a 'There you are, Ms Feldman. Have a very good day.' He was Asian, a gentle man, who took his role as sub-postmaster to be a social service, and made a point of treating his customers as individuals. Most local people appreciated it, and didn't mind waiting a few extra moments in the queue while he had a pleasant chat with the old lady in front.

Bella pulled her cardigan tighter around her and re-folded her arms in front of it. She did not want to go out, to see people in the street, to be greeted as Leah by the kindly sub-postmaster (he had become more familiar over the past few months) when she handed over her giro cheque. It was late November and it wasn't going to get any warmer, but perhaps it wouldn't get any colder either for a day or two. She could manage it as it was. She didn't care about discomfort, it was distraction she had to avoid. It couldn't be helped about Mel needing money; she wouldn't have bothered her upstairs neighbour unnecessarily. No one did, they let her alone for the most part. It was the sound of 'Leah' with 'Feldman' falling silently into place beside it – intended by Mel as normal and friendly, she knew – that she found so distressing. Diverting her, calling back feelings and memories like an old song half heard on a passing car radio, and sticking in the air, evoking the flavour of another time, another world.

Leah had just missed being born and living all her life in a

Russian *shtetl*. She was never equipped by her parents, who *had* come from the Old Country, for a life so modern and dismally eventful as hers turned out to be. Perhaps, even, there was something of the Old Country ways in her blood which prevented her from coming to terms with the modern world's disorder, or its disrespect for a simple order that looked like fairness. She was born into grim urban poverty in the East End of London, but also into all the anticipation which life in a new country affords. For her, and her family, that meant making a good match. The boys might look to learning and education to get themselves beyond their parents' limited horizons, but the girls married well if they could – in the *shtetl* to scholars, merchants and rabbis – to change their lives. Leah could only hope for a good marriage, but those options – severely limited in scope in the small world of the *shtetl* – were vastly multiplied in a great metropolis where all kinds lived cheek by jowl, and the wildest girlish daydreams really did sometimes come true.

Leah dreamed with the best of them. Her mother died when she was eight years old, leaving nothing but a faded oval sepia photograph of a young beauty sitting in a troika. Where and how she came to be sitting in it, and photographed looking so delicate and *Russian*, Leah had no idea. But whatever dreams the photograph represented to the young woman had faded into marriage with a local boy whose prospects were no better than her own. The beauty failed, for some reason, to bring her mother the marriage that would change her family's life. Perhaps it was a kind of beauty that could only be perceived by a future generation.

Leah's father had used up all his physical and mental resources in making the journey to England. Perhaps he had had very few to start with. They settled in a tenement in Stepney's Brick Lane and thereafter he devoted himself to a lifetime of drinking tea and giving vent to sullen rage. He was violent, beating his wife when the disappointment – what disappointment, Leah had wondered as a child; could he ever possibly have had dreams? – overcame him, using a sturdy leather strap on the children whenever they made their presence known. When her mother died, Leah took over as the woman of the household, cleaning, cooking, keeping the little kids in some kind of order and out of their father's way. It was the end of her elementary schooling. She could just about read and write. All that was left of her childlife were daydreams and wishes. Wishes that her mother hadn't died, leaving her without the love and comfort she thought she remembered receiving. Daydreams that something would take her out of the misery of Brick Lane and into a world of glamour, pictured everywhere, devoid of want – though as a child, the fantasized glamour consisted simply of the dream of not being frightened that there wasn't enough money to buy food.

Dreams coming true, or seeming to come true, are sometimes lethal – at the least a reliable cause of human heartbreak. Leah went on dreaming, while her father sank further into his morose silence, sitting forever in front of the fire, hitting out occasionally when his food or tea failed to arrive according to his whim. There were a few local boys, some of whom offered Leah marriage – she was a pretty young woman, like her mother had been – but none of them seemed to hold out the prospect of change and a better life. At twenty she met Ray in a local café. He was visiting his parents, having already made a life for himself out in the real world away from the dark, impoverished streets of the East End. He was 'in business', though he didn't specify, and clearly the business was going well, if his smart suit, shiny shoes and snappy hat were anything to go by. He looked a world away from the other boys she knew, and it was a world Leah ached to be part of. She ran off with Ray, leaving her father and the kids early one morning without a qualm, and they married in a whirl of excitement.

There were good times, at first. Leah expressed her dreams with the good things money could buy. They went abroad, to Monte Carlo, to Nice. They had a child. Ray went into property, buying and selling houses, and made enough for Leah finally to feel certain that she would never have to worry about having food again. Indeed, the only concern she had was how long it would be before she could exchange her full-length Persian Lamb coat for a mink. She had never heard of fortune reversing itself, or of dreams draining away, so it never occurred to her to worry. She and Ray were even happy for the first few years. Happy enough.

Certainly, there were arguments; she was spending more than he was bringing in and he came back once or twice with rouge or powder on the collar of his shirt. They would shout at each other and slam doors. As panic mixed with disappointment welled up in her and she began to see how narrow her options were, Leah developed a tendency to emotional melodrama, and with each domestic difficulty it expanded inside her until every argument and any setback became the 'end of her life' and her whole existence – as if it were a concrete building hit by an earthquake – was ruined utterly and forever, destroyed, and there was nothing left to do but kill herself. Nothing, nothing. She screamed a good deal and then sank into a sulky, desolated silence.

Leah did what she had done in her father's house, cooked and cleaned and looked after Miriam, though now she was doing it for herself, and the objects of her attention were her own. It never occurred to her to finish her education, though Ray had been to grammar school, and could, if he'd wanted, have gone to university. It never occurred to her to get a job. Married women didn't need careers then, and the whole point of the dream coming true was that she would be looked after by a capable and doting man. She never thought of the future, beyond the next rise in her standard of living, because her future was now settled so far as she was concerned. She was out of the *shtetl* and in society. She had achieved everything she had dreamed of in life. Of course, her dreams were limited by the times and her original degree of impoverishment, but she couldn't know that.

That Leah Feldman was distant, a stranger to Bella. If someone had stopped in the street and called out 'Leah Feldman? Is that you?' (but who would?) she would not have turned around, or even slowed her pace. But Leah Feldman was an *intimate* stranger whose summoning-up at the sound of her name came complete with a life of her own. Not Bella's, for Bella's life was relatively recent. Even so, she was disturbed by alien memories she wanted nothing more to do with. Memories, like other people, were distraction. The proper task was to exist in the immediate moment. Memories of long ago were fiendish sprites determined to undermine her struggle to stay true to the present.

Bella returned to her table and the open bible, but still, though her eyes read the print, no words would form in her mouth. Bella huddled, still stalled over her half-uttered psalm. The present was silent.

For a while, during the transition between being Leah and becoming Bella, many months in reality, Leah had loitered in a no-man's land. The world turned fuzzy at the edges of her vision, and became entirely transparent at the centre. No doubt the drugs they gave her had something to do with it, but essentially Leah took leave of absence. It was possible to stare straight ahead at nothing, she discovered, without the slightest sense that she should be doing anything else, her mind as empty as the world she failed to perceive. There were no thoughts, only a gentle trickling inside herself, as if a plug had been pulled out and her substance was draining away. When it had entirely gone, very gradually thought of a sort intruded, or rather images. The emptiness her drained substance left behind, transformed from nothing into a blasted landscape which existed both inside her and out. It was something, though it did not, at first, require her attention.

The barren landscape which developed in her interior space was vast and undifferentiated, with no boundaries, nor any regions, because it had no architecture of time. It developed only in immensity, tending as the weeks and months passed, towards the absolute; or perhaps, rather than itself evolving, it was Leah who developed an understanding of its essentially absolute nature. Unbounded and without signposts, this empty panorama became Leah's reality. She did not feel hard done by, or cheated of life any longer. She felt safe in what had become her normality, and the growing, anguishing loneliness that was the air of her wilderness seemed to be a part of the normality. This reality, at least, could be relied on not to disappoint, not to fall apart and leave her in the lurch. Her hysteria and panic fell away into a curious calm. She became another person entirely.

But the loneliness was not content to remain just a passive corollary of the great space inside her. It had a life of its own. The loneliness began to *hunger*. It wanted something, feeling itself as a lack. It wanted to remain itself, as all things want to remain themselves, but it desired its cause. It became Leah's shadow, a dark shape which though essentially her, pulled towards something positive in an attempt to escape its intolerable negativity. In making her uncomfortable, it separated itself from her, setting itself against her passive acceptance of the seamless desert, and made demands. Incomprehensible demands, to Leah, who found a longing in herself and had no idea to what it tended, to what it could possibly tend in the world around her of which she was no longer part. The pain of it was one thing; the bafflement another.

Like someone suffering from physical hunger, she had, eventually, to look around for what food might be available to assuage the discomfort. She began to return to the world, though with her wilderness intact. Now she was merely a pair of eyes and a vehicle for something in her that refused to let her continue to sit and stare in the comfort of the asylum. The new woman who emerged from hospital nine months after she was carried into it from some anonymous street, was empty, emotionally quiescent, and back in a world which she had to negotiate without any of the assumptions of her past. The husband, the child, she once had were immensely distant, irrelevant, forgotten, part of an amorphous past which had once contained pain. Only the present moment counted, she had learned. Get through the present moment, then there would be another one. Get through that. Time moved step by very small step, as her body did. There were no more wishes and no place in a continuous present for dreams. It made life easier and much quieter. Her thinking became clearer as if her previous life had been the education she seemed to have lacked, but which now finally had taken. The shadow longing, the underbelly of loneliness, did not go away. It stayed and endured her existence with her. It was, perhaps, her only friend.

73

She made no attempt to re-assert herself as Miriam's mother. She had walked out in a maelstrom of confusion, but when a calmer frame of mind descended, with the help of the drugs, she concluded that it would be best if she remained vanished. Quite apart from the odd, alien feeling she had about her past, she could quite see that Miriam would be better off without her – even if it was not a proper or conventional arrangement. The proper and conventional were no longer part of Leah's concerns. It was as if she had died, and Miriam's continued absence confirmed that feeling. Her loneliness needed an assurance that it could remain what it was. It might hanker for something, but hankering was its nature – it was not after anything as real as a growing daughter. She was, of course, identified, but she made it clear that she would have nothing to do with the past, and the psychologists, in consultation with Miriam's foster parents, decided, for better or worse, to let the situation rest as it was. If Miriam asked any direct questions about her mother, it was agreed that she would be told. But Miriam seemed content to put the past behind her.

When the time came for Leah to go out into the world, it was a birth into the unknown. Leah began her new existence with something close to the minimal baggage of a new-born. Nothing from the past came along with her. The furniture and Persian Lamb coat had been sold off to take care of her unpaid bills. There was just her new self, a handful of clothes bought for her from the hospital fund, and a rented room the medical social worker had arranged along with the state benefit she was entitled to as a single, unemployed woman with neither savings nor property to fall back on.

And about her name, she decided, something must be done. She was no longer Leah Feldman. That person being long gone, it seemed inappropriate, even dishonest, to retain the name. She had to keep it for official purposes, but for herself and any future enquirers she needed something else. The name 'Bella' came to mind, for no reason, and for just that lack of reason she adopted it. She did not have the heart to invent a last name. She felt it would make her too substantial. Feldman remained on her payment book, but there was no need, if any non-official person asked, to give them more than Bella. From time to time when a surname was insisted on she said just whatever came out of her mouth. Only once, that time with Mel on the stairs, had this technique failed her, and *Leah* had risen, unbidden, and by then she felt, inaccurately, to her lips.

Bella had settled into her room and found it a satisfying match to her interior desolation. The longing moved in, too. She lived through empty days and weeks with it in a listening silence, trying, though not too energetically, to discover what it might be longing for. She needed a way to continue to exist, which meant finding a way, not to extinguish the pain, which she knew was too difficult and probably undesirable, but to incorporate it into her continued existence and to give it something in the way of nourishment. Eventually, she linked her unquenched longing to an ache for something more than anything to be found in the world. She acknowledged the ache to be a desiring of the spirit, not the body.

But what could a woman devoid of a past and passive as to the future manage in the way of nourishment for the spirit? Belief was out of the question. There was nothing to believe in without the sense of an ongoing story, either private or public. Her vacancy could not admit a purpose in either sphere.

Gradually she came up with a notion which seemed to make sense both to her desolate self and her shadow self. A terrible sort of sense, admittedly, but there was no other kind. If she could not give herself up to *belief*, she could commit herself, perhaps, to *faith*, objectless, naked, and bereft of narrative, but all the more powerful, it may be, for that.

Wasn't that, after all, what the hunger was? A desire for faith, for a reaching out towards something outside herself which nonetheless did not connect her categorically to a world she had no wish to be a part of? To have faith in what she had no belief in was, for such a woman, audacious, and yet perfect in some way that true believing could never be, tainted as it was by wishes and fantasies of redemption. She dismissed Judaism as too embedded in the details of everyday life, and too close to her former self, and chose, instead, the structure of Catholicism for its ritualistic abstraction, for its rites and repetitions, like scaffolding for climbers with no handhold on glacial reality. She entered the church in precise opposition to her earlier entrance into St Martin's-in-the-Fields. Leah Feldman had gone in, in search of supernatural consolation for the emptiness and disappointment of her life. She had stood in the darkened aisle, facing the paraphernalia of credulity, reaching out to it in the hope that it might reach out to her. She had heard of such – what might they be called? – miracles, acts of grace? In St Martin's-in-the-Fields, she had offered up her despair and waited for something to happen. In the event, not even the human arm of religion in the form of a priest had come to her aid. This time, however, Bella entered the church void of expectation and hope, to make of its shell the enclosing outline of her precious wilderness.

She spent some months slipping into dark churches to attend services to see what might be made of the notion of faith without belief. What she saw and heard confirmed the fitness of her choice.

'As it was in the beginning . . .' she sub-vocalized with the scattered smatterings of congregations, learning as she went along. And the words did no violence to the emptiness inside her. '. . . is now and ever shall be, world without end.' She studied the Bible and with new-found cunning discovered intricate alleyways between the wide paths of righteousness where she could make her own stealthy way. 'In the beginning was the Word, and the Word was with God, and the Word was God.' God was not God. The name of God was God. The Word was God. God was the Word. If she spoke it, she spoke not of God, a pre-existent being, but created God, stated God into being for no more than the length of a monosyllable passing through her lips and dying in the air of the world. Each naming – God. God. God. – was a resurrection and a dying of nothingness into nothingness. A brief being of non-being. World without end. The mystery of the death and resurrection was the secret of the world without end. The endless

76

repetition of the Word, re-creating the world, empty, meaning-less, but without end.

As it was in the beginning. This was not comfort, but a statement of endurance. The past was the present, persisting unalterable, . minute by minute, a stating of the Word, of having to create God continually over and over again, knowing His absolute non-existence to be the single truth that was unchangeable both in beginning and now, for ever and ever, world without end. *Our Father, who art in heaven.* There was no father and no heaven. The obligation was to say the prayer every single day, and to get up the next and the next, to say it with perfect faith but equally perfect unbelief. *Hallowed be thy name.* The name I give you: *God*, the Word that brings about the object of the perfect unbelief for a fraction of a second. *This is my body. This is my blood.* Eat the wafer, sip the wine, say the words – ingest the substance of the utterly insubstantial. Believe in the wafer and the wine, though not in their transubstantiation, for there is no substance, there can be no transformation in a stationary world without end. Believe in this with all your heart and soul and mind. Body and blood without end. Without beginning. Continuing. The great circular empty space. *World without end. Amen. So be it.*

She devoted herself to the Gospel of John. Only in the Gospel of John did Christ cry out at the end: *My God, my God, why hast thou forsaken me?* And only in the Gospel of John is the Word the beginning. The death of Christ was the end of the world; the moment when the Word no longer worked. *My God, my God.* Christ's loss of faith in the monosyllable brought death. His inability to resurrect God through the Word was the moment of extinction of the world. Ever after, man had to resurrect Christ and the world by reciting God back into a myriad of infinitesimal existences. And this was the redemption. Christ failed so that we might live. The real trinity was Emptiness, Failure and the Word – that holy, ghostly, meaningless monosyllable. The non-existent, non-substance which must be invoked and faced without flinch-ing, day in, day out. *I believe in the Father, Son and Holy Spirit.* It must be said, again and again. *I believe (though I do not believe).*

Light candles, sink to your knees, follow the creed. Create God in order that in the momentary creation you make the space for a fleeting existence of your own. A pinpoint when you can say, 'This is where I am,' though it is in no way different from anywhere else in the featureless landscape. There is still no direction or destination, but there comes to be a series of identical points of reference that are essentially without meaning because they exist outside time, which provide an intermittent sense of the present moment which both creator and created hunger for.

So Bella, formerly Leah, née Feldman, further now into the abstract than she had ever imagined in the old material life, was received into the Catholic Church. She took instruction from a local priest who welcomed her conversion from the old faith to the true faith, and explained with gentle care and attention the meaning of the rites and rituals of the Holy Church. He baptized her, and they continued to meet as he became more and more convinced that she had a vocation. She did not speak of her wilderness, nor how faith devoid of belief fitted into it, but he felt in her a fervour that was quiet and absolutely certain, and of a strength he could hardly remember encountering before. He was not surprised when she first used the word 'vocation'; it had been on the tip of his tongue for some months. Bella did not want to deceive her priest, but she did not tell him the whole truth about the nature of her belief, since she was sure that *his* faith was quite different and he would not be able to understand that her sincerity was no less for her lack of belief in God. He could say, 'Christ died for our sins' and mean that God had sent his only son, divinity incarnate, to suffer human life and death in order to accomplish human redemption. He heard the words of the Church with the ear of belief, and they always made sense to him. As Bella learned the language and dogma of the Church it became easier to speak the words that would work for the priest. She did not flinch from saying what she did not believe to be true, because the truth was inviolable and was created by the Word, spoken in defiance of disbelief. *The Word* could not be diminished by mere insincerity. And, in any case, everything she said was shadowed by its underlying truth. *World without end (world with endless non-endings). I believe (though I do not believe). Forgive us our trespasses (you who do not exist and cannot forgive what we cannot have trespassed against). In the beginning God created the heavens and the earth (World without beginning, world without end). And the earth was without form, and void; and darkness was upon the face of the deep (Yes, yes, oh yes).* She did have a vocation. It was a driving need to find a shape and space for her wilderness, a geometry, to place herself within it, and to devote her days to its blank, black mystery.

While she listened to the Church's teaching as it was filtered through Father Michael, simple, straightforward, reasonable in the demands it made of believers, and modest in the face of the majesty of God, she also, without mentioning it to her mentor, came upon the work of Martin Buber, who thundered faith into her ears. There was nothing liberal about Buber, no compromising nonsense about the God-within-us-all. His God was actual and other, utterly outside our sphere of understanding, beyond our comprehension, but an existent Being, a Person, a solid Thou to Bella's insubstantial I. Buber's Old Testament God was to be confronted, like a child walking into the darkness knowing its parent to be there, the knowledge not the seeing being enough to keep it walking through the absence of light. *Over against us*, Buber kept saying. Like darkness, God was immensely, invisibly there, though not here, not some part of the individual who, looking inside his own heart, discovers himself to be divine. Only God is divine, and God is not Bella. The task was to strive to come close to the unknowable, to consent to its wishes, to allow its work in us to occur. Bella was drawn to this dark and lonely vision, though, of course, she did not believe in this other, fearsome God, any more than she believed in God the Father, the kindly old gentleman. But it confirmed her sense that to strive for the unreachable, to believe in the impossible, to contemplate the non-existent and the incomprehensible was the only way to survive the rest of her life. Her lack of belief was to be the anchor of her faith.

With the blessing of Father Michael she became a postulant in the order of the Poor Clares, and in six months was accepted as a novice in the convent he suggested might best suit her vocation.

For three years Bella served the God she did not believe in with prayer, ritual, and much polishing of furniture and scrubbing of floors. She found none of these things boring or arduous or pointless, but cherished them for the opportunities for vacancy they afforded. It was the community life she found difficult. Serving God required tolerance and generosity towards the other sisters in the dangerously small and isolated community. They prayed together, gardened together, sewed together, recreated together and ate together. Whereas the absence of meaning she was searching for could be found in the courage of empty prayer, living with others in God's love could not be part of the emotional vacuum she was trying to create for herself. Her courage and perversity did not extend that far. The daily life of the convent dripped with community and meaningful exchanges between its members. The smiling nod of recognition as they passed each other on the stairs was an intolerable assault on her solitary wilderness. It afforded no hiding place for Bella who, try though she might to find a surface complicity, could not help but seem distant from her sisters.

The Novice Mistress spoke often to her about her apparent aloofness.

'We serve Christ in love,' she said to Sister Boniface. 'We must express this as love for one another.'

'I have never exchanged a cross word with anyone, Sister,' Sister Boniface said.

'No, you are a model of control. But I'm afraid it shows. The sisters find you remote, some are even frightened of you. Sometimes, I am frightened of you.'

'It's just my manner, Sister.'

She was given the most humble and menial jobs in an attempt to correct this manner of hers, but the very meticulousness with which they were carried out, the careful deference with which she treated the most junior of the sisters only managed to convey her distance from them.

Everyone, of course, got irritated and short tempered from time to time, living so close as they did. There were individuals who rubbed up against the others, and one or two who seemed to have been born in order to annoy, but Sister Boniface was different. There was never a human loss of composure, only a strict politeness which seemed to be what served in her for an approximation – for which they were all trying – of Christ's love. There was no warmth. Even those who annoyed their sisters could be said to be bestowing a gift on them – the chance to pray for strength and tolerance and to love the irritating one in spite of whatever it was that got under the skin. Sister Boniface gave nothing while appearing to give her all.

Her confessor brought the matter up often enough, but no amount of Hail Marys or penances seemed to make very much difference. Sister Boniface was just not a natural member of an enclosed convent or any other community of souls.

'Father,' she said to her confessor after a couple of years, 'perhaps I don't have a vocation for religious life in a community. But haven't there been people who have lived a solitary life dedicated to God? Hermits lived alone, but were living in Christ. Do they still exist? Couldn't I be a hermit?'

Father Sullivan met her request with a look of severe disapproval, distaste even.

'The vocation to lead the life of a hermit within the Church is a very rare and special gift. It is not done lightly, Sister, just to get away from the difficulty of living with others. On the contrary, those very few souls with such a vocation have fought and prayed against it until they understood there was no alternative for them. You can't escape from the difficulties of the world into the solitary life; the Church is not there for that. Withdrawal was not Christ's way. Hermits have a purpose in the world. They do not turn their back on life, no matter how it looks. Your most important task is to temper your belief with humility towards your sisters.'

But Father Sullivan was as deceived as everyone else about Sister Boniface's problem. At the core of it was not just the sister's lack of social skills, but her empty, though none-the-less profound faith. Probably she prayed more, meditated harder and genuflected with greater deliberation than the others, but she lacked the simplicity and delight of their belief, their utter conviction, and it showed in the separation, the difference the others felt in her. It didn't occur to anyone to doubt her sincerity, no one guessed the true nature of her convoluted commitment to what she had no belief in, but the vacuum in her heart, in her soul, was the source of the unease which spread about her through the convent, like ripples in a still pool into which a stone is dropped. They admired her piety and continuous study of the Bible, but even the barely literate Sister Joseph had more real understanding of the meaning of the love of Christ than Sister Boniface, though her words were monosyllabic and came only with scarlet-faced difficulty. When Sister Joseph said 'Praise the Lord!' as she pulled an onion from the soil for the stewpot, she had an exact idea of who she was praising and why; and her praises were all the more joyful for being entirely unquestioned. Sister Boniface's murmured hallelujahs when she lifted an onion were a screen for the blankness behind the words, a mere exercise in the exercise of faith.

It became increasingly clear that Sister Boniface would not spend an easy lifetime as a nun, growing old and fat in the daily round of devotions, and, more troubling, nor would the other sisters find the living easy while she remained in the convent.

Perhaps, it was suggested by the Novice Mistress, Father Sullivan and finally the Mother herself, she was better suited to teaching, and to pursuing, under the aegis of the Church, a less contemplative life. Still a nun, of course – her piety was not in doubt – but a different, less enclosed and contemplative order might be the best thing. But it was the enclosure and contemplation which Sister Boniface wanted. She read of the desert fathers and their solitary struggles in the vacant deserts of the world with the desert in their hearts, their arid battles against doubt and emptiness, their deliberate confinement of themselves away from society to confront the blackness and unknowability of an unpicturable, unpraisable, infinite, infinitely strange God. This was the God for Sister Boniface: a negation, and then a negation of a negation. A God who was a vast, unbounded wasteland into which one hurled one's aimless faith and expected nothing but bleak emptiness to echo through the blackness in return.

She rejected all attempts to find her some more suitable place to exist within the Church. Eventually, it was clear that she would not be allowed to take her vows, especially since obedience was the essence of those vows, and when all possible avenues, barring staying where she was, had been explored and rejected, she agreed after three years as a novice to give up her vocation as a nun.

Or so she said to Father Sullivan and the Mother Superior of her convent. In her heart, she gave the Church up and maintained her vocation. The day she left the convent with fifty pounds and an address of a Catholic half-way house, she took her own vows of poverty, chastity and obedience.

The achievable reality of poverty and chastity presented no problem; they were only too easy to incorporate into her life. The question which arose was to whom or what she was to be obedient. The answer spoke itself for all those not deafened by the theology of the Church. She would be obedient to poverty and chastity. The vows were self-inclusive, a circular promise to live in practical and necessary obedience to the simplest of living, so that she might be free to give her final obedience to the God of unbelief, to be as near in kind and spirit as she might come to the unlit absence of her desert – that great and terrible simplicity.

It was not necessary to find an actual desert. Desolation came naturally from her current state of destitution. She tore up the address of the sympathetically religious half-way house and became a person with fifty pounds, the clothes she stood up in, and nowhere to live. A second rebirth.

She wandered through the streets of London in search of a place for herself, and speaking to some of those she came across, soon learned to register herself as homeless with the local social-security office who told her that she could receive benefit only if she had an address, and handed her a list of hostels. She went to the first, was given a room on the top floor and told to register the following morning back at social security so that she might receive her rent.

Finding her place in the world seemed to be as easy as following her destiny. She had a room, starker than her cell at the convent in its tawdriness: empty of all comfort, even parodying comfort with a threadbare patch of pale green carpet mocking itself for a rug, a chair that had never been quite easy, but was now derelict, its cushions bleeding wedges of foam from slashed brownish fabric, and wooden arms at either side, their veneered strips curling back on themselves, defying any arm to take its rest upon them. In one corner a chipped and filthy butler sink harboured months, maybe years, of uncleared grease around its sides, while water dripped from a washerless tap, already weathering a dent where it fell. This sink served for washing, or the splash or two that kept Bella next to godliness in her current fashion, and provided the holy water with which she anointed her forehead and lips from her only teacup as she whispered '*In the name of the Father, and of the Son and of the Holy Ghost . . . as it was in the beginning, is now and ever shall be, world without end. Amen.*'

Each evening she fed enough coins into the meter to allow the gas fire to dance for a brief hour in the darkness. A sort of luxury, as were the candles she purchased out of her giro, one for every other day of the week, which she lit and allowed to burn half-way down each evening before she extinguished it and plunged herself into the night of darkness which was more in keeping with the pattern of her daily reality. She spent a basic minimum on bread, cheese and milk, her regular sustenance, and managed to find warm, woollen clothing – it was winter now and cooling fast – at church jumble sales. A few pence for a well-worn cardigan, almost waterproof shoes, a torn but serviceable coat. In the matter of clothing, for a person of limited means who wasn't planning to go anywhere stylish, the Church had its uses, she acknowledged.

No one in the house had more than a room and the bare necessities of life, though they all knew how easy it was to have less. To have a giro-cheque and a place to sleep, not clean, not exactly waterproof, certainly not warm, but inside for all that, counted for something. It was more than nothing, and there were plenty of people with that, who had slipped from where they themselves at least were, to testify that more than nothing is something to be grateful for. Well, not grateful for, but glad of.

Bella lived as one of them, angrily and happily, after her fashion, though she kept herself to herself. Her days were paced according to the timing of the Divine Office, as it had been said at the convent. A strict timetable of alternating prayer and silence segmented the day, marking its passage from dawn to dusk. '*Keep us in this night* . . .' The voiced prayer and the intervening silence were like a tidal sea, rolling in on the wave of her devotions and rolling out to her meditations on the vacant silences they left behind. Those quiet periods drained the sound from what had gone before, dismissing the shadow of the psalms of praise and supplication she had vocalized. The silence was the aural equivalent of the darkness into which she spoke, to the nothing-ness to which her ironic praises were directed. She believed in no Father, Son or Holy Ghost, and with utter conviction gave thanks to the empty silence that would descend as soon as the sound of her voice had died away.

Unlike at the convent there was no actual work to do beyond the ordinary business of surviving. It turned out that life in a condition of continued unemployment in a country which had the remnants of a welfare state was closer to the enclosed religious ideal than any convent could provide. Life was marked by the exigencies of poverty. Getting the wherewithal to stay alive required considerable attention; the State did not provide for its indigents without requiring them to make an appropriate effort, and what it did provide was not designed to be excessive – though it did, in Bella's case (having no children or unpaid debts) allow for the purchase, for example, of those seven candles a fortnight. It was hardship only in the sense that there were those had more, but it would have been harder with nothing. Here she was being supported while living the life of a religious – though not because of that: she was supported because she was supposed to be inadequate. In fact, though she did not argue with the assumptions the authorities made, she was living the most nearly adequate life she had ever lived.

To say Bella was angry was not to say that she either experienced or conveyed anger. She was angry, but she did not feel it. She felt nothing; only the passing of her days in periods of prayer and devotion. But her essential condition was anger, as it had always been. If ever she had been innocent, which is to say a time prior to anger, it would have been for a very brief period, for the short time when it is possible not to know the pain that others can inflict by their stupidity or neglect or their departure from the world before one has received enough of whatever it is that makes the world a safe and tolerable place. Once others are recognized, or recognized as absent, and their capacity for pain-giving becomes evident, there is no longer innocence. After that, everything is a lie and a subterfuge, because all that concerns the soul struggling to survive is its survival, and all its energies are taken up with the self-deception and fantasy which is made necessary by the controlling others. The choice seemed to be, at a very early stage, to live in a miasma of fear or dangerously to dream. Both the fear and the dreaming had led her to uncontrollable hysteria; great noise, great energy always lacking a desired outcome.

Now, after exploring the hysteria to its fullest, most life-stopping extent and finding herself vacated, she had discovered a new way: to live only in the moment. This happened, then that happened, but she never allowed the idea that 'this might be going to happen' or 'it might not'. She pretended to others, when necessary, a past and future, but learned to live only within the current intake or outflow of breath. It put a fence around fear, and it allowed her quietly to develop her own cosmology which might look very like the one the world around her endorsed, but which belonged outside all systems depending on time. Her God, her absent Friend, was a creature only of the present, created by her, utterly controlled by her, moment by moment. Behind her single-minded devotion to this Friend was an unspoken, unthought, threat or choice: the possibility of refraining from re-inventing the moment and thereby causing her creation (and in the process, herself – the creation of her creation) to fail to resurrect. It, she, they could, at any second of her choosing, go out. Like a light.

All this, this whole new life's work, was born out of anger, the desire to punish a life whose devotion to material dreams had caused such misery, such disappointment. He, God, would pay for his neglect by becoming her creature, her invention. She dreamed up a deity who depended entirely on her prayers and her praises for his existence.

Of course, the others in the house thought she was close to mad, though not dangerous. She did not let them know about her vocation, but there was something so *concentrated*, so *concealed* about her, that only madness could account for it. She muttered to herself a good deal, passing people on the stairs or on the street, and though they were prayers she muttered, angrily, under her breath, to revive God and remind him that he was her object, she looked to Mel and the others in the house, like a shabby, lonely, pathetic wreck of a woman talking to herself.

But Mel liked Bella for all that, in a distant kind of way, and treated her when they met, as normally as possible. After all, from Mel's point of view, there wasn't much to be found between the officially sane and the marginally mad, except it seemed to be the task of the sane ones to make life as difficult as possible for her and her boy to get on. Bella didn't hinder or seem to make judgements; and she would help out with money if she had it. And if today she didn't want to talk, well, so what? Sometimes Mel didn't want to talk either, and sometimes she just wanted to lie in her bed, under the skimpy blankets and howl her fucking eyes out. Couldn't, of course, because it would frighten the boy. Maybe, one of these days, when Bella was not playing dumb, Mel would ask her to look after him for an hour so she could have a good cry.

★

87

But today, in fact, Bella's silence was anything but willed. However much she tried to throw Psalm 137 in God the Deceiver's face, her tongue cleaved to the roof of her mouth.

> *. . . If I do not remember thee, let my tongue cleave to the roof of my mouth . . .*

She was afflicted with silence. The words would not be spoken; the Word would not be uttered. Her mouth was bone dry, her throat constricted and aching with the effort to speak. What hold had she over her creator if she could not speak the Word that brought him into existence? Without a voice there was no word, and without the Word where was the world? Where was she? Uncreated, deserted by the deserter, her wilderness narrowed to the margins of her physical being. With no inside, and outside merely a desolation, there was nowhere for the boundless desert her sullen being needed for its existence.

She closed her bible and the silence became all the greater as she sat on, suddenly without a present. The past and the future grew in front of her eyes like mould on an ancient, neglected ruin. Her present in ruins, her past and future rising up like wraiths, monstrously limiting, in its absence.

> *By the rivers of Babylon, there we sat down, yea, we wept . . .*

And Bella wept, silent tears streaming like a river overrunning its banks, down her cheeks, there on her wooden chair with her hands folded, without cunning, in her lap.

> *How shall we sing the Lord's song in a strange land?*

4

Mimi had woken late the following morning without Jack to disturb her as he left for work. She opened her eyes to the accomplished fact of Jack having gone. The idea held no surprise for her, as might have been expected of a person awakening to very new and very different circumstances. There was no fleeting moment when, coming to consciousness, she looked for Jack lying beside her in the bed and then remembered what had happened. She did not have to replay the details of that night to make her new circumstances seem real. She woke knowing Jack was not there and was not going to be there again – except, of course, to pick up the rest of his things in the fullness of time. She was neither surprised nor unduly distressed by this fact, since she woke also to the knowledge that Jack's former presence and present absence was merely a necessary but not a sufficient condition for the new kind of life she had decided to lead. What had been wrong all this time, Mimi had at last realized, was that she had been fighting a vocation. She might, she thought, devote the rest of her days to staying in bed.

Now, in the solitary morning after their visit to the cinema, the late-night coupling and Jack's departure, Mimi curled herself into a ball under the duvet and slid her hand between her thighs, pressing her palm gently against her vulva as if to comfort it, as one would hold in a steady embrace a small child being deceived by adults. Knowing no better, innocent that it was, it was damp and ready for her touch, primed by her memory, still receptive from the sex of a few hours before, stimulated even – perhaps especially – by the thought of the unknown sex Jack had had before he came home. Her pitying palm relented and slowly began to massage the tingling labia open. She flooded away thought with the remembered sound of Jack groaning in her ear – and before, in another ear – and let her throat mimic it, until imitation became the thing itself; the low, moaning sound of her own pleasure as her fricating palm rocked her into orgasm.

A new day had begun. But Mimi in her new horizontal mode felt no sense of urgency about participating in it, and allowed it to go its own way. She concentrated instead on the diminishing waves within her as her climax wound down. Soon, after the initial crack and crash, the swell of her desire impacted more softly with her enclosing boundaries, until it was just sloshing gently to and fro in the whisper of wind which was all that remained of the tempest she had whipped up in herself. As the drama let up, Mimi wondered if this wasn't what she liked best; the unravelling of the extreme moment of tension into an almost hallucinatory calm. Soft, kindly rhythms rippled through her, defining her centre by extending themselves into her extremities, passing like oil in water through her thighs and shoulders, into her calves and forearms, finding the very edges of herself before doubling back to make their slow oleaginous return. Back at her centre, a precise interior location between her navel and vagina, her pleasure folded itself away neatly, a nugget of hiatus, undiminished by the pleasing residue it had left behind in the rest of her softly singing body.

Jack, and the exciting cause of her current gratification, were quite forgotten as Mimi lay sprawled and liquid-muscled in bed. There was nothing but sensation and its after-effects, to which she willingly submitted in a self-induced trance of well-being. She wondered idly what the time was and supposed vaguely she'd better get up, but her body couldn't have been further from the thought. If Jack were here, that is if Jack had brought her to this state rather than herself, he would, round about now have murmured a gratified 'Mmm . . .' and asked, 'Want a cigarette?' Or she might have broken the moment herself and reached up to stroke his wayward hair, or lifted her head from his chest and planted a soft kiss on his lips. Unless they fell asleep, the silence after their sex together, as with most people, she supposed, was quite quickly breached by one or other of them making a bid for reassuring connection. Reassuring to whom? Of what? Somehow, after orgasm it was necessary to acknowledge the other person, to let them know that you were still there, to check that they also remained, as if the journey each travelled might have taken them quite away from the person they clung to so tightly, whose name they called out, whose body dripped with their mingled sweat. But this was what she liked best: to be alone to savour without interruption (or the need to interrupt) the last, lingering vestiges of a sexual moment. She never wanted to be wrenched out of her privacy. At first with Jack, as with others, she had turned away after it was over and curled up with her back to him, letting herself sink into her own sensations. Jack, and the others, had resented it; asking her at first what the matter was, and subsequently placing a restricting arm around her as she started to move away, pulling her close and face to face with him. Her pulling away and murmured, inadequate responses were not acceptable. Not wanting to offend, or not feeling free to pursue her own inclinations, she made herself stay connected and available to Jack, but often, she would remain in bed for a while after he had left for work and treat herself to the unsocial pleasure of private orgasm. Which was why today did not seem very particular.

Mimi drifted between her orgasm-induced half-sleep and the closing throb of her uterus, while conscientiously keeping a small segment of herself alert. This was part of the sexual pleasure – or the pleasure of sex: to remain aware of everything her body did for her or in spite of her; to acknowledge every slide towards unconsciousness and every thrum. If she had fallen asleep, or allowed the physical signs of relief and release to pass unnoticed, much of the point of the experience would have been wasted. If she could have she'd have taken account of the life of every separate cell in her body. The delights of the flesh could only be fully appreciated by a watchful mind. They had to be *minded* to be properly enjoyed. The trick was to allow the body to drift off in its own way, but not to let it actually escape the attention of the observing mind. It would have been only half the pleasure to have allowed herself to go fully into sleep with her mind no longer available to enjoy it. It was a slippery balance, and not one she could achieve with a spent lover beside her, and particularly not Jack, who, spent or not, was dedicated to filling empty spaces with whatever, or whoever, was to hand.

It was astonishing that she should have chosen and been chosen by Jack. It was not astonishing that their relationship should now have come to its end. If Mimi was living out the theory that opposites attract, then she had in the process discovered an amendment which suggested that if opposites do attract they do not do so for long. Even with its practical rider the theory had the obviousness of much popular sociology, and was not, to Mimi's mind, very helpful in solving the mystery she had found herself living in for the past three years.

There was never a moment when she hadn't wondered 'What am I doing with this man?', but the nature of the question altered with the passing of time. At first, the wrongness worked a spell for her. She allowed his wrongness to delight and excite her. Later, there was something more solemn, even ominous in her question. Finally, there was the panic of a small girl-child lost in the woods. Given that their time together was over, there was, perhaps, no need for Mimi to see the relationship as anything more than a mistake. An episode. An error that everyone makes, and she made less often than most. But the mystery overwhelmed the wrongness for her. The 'How could I?' quite overrode 'That was a mistake.' She was left with questions that needed answering, though she couldn't see quite why they did.

It was Jack's intense sense of urgency, which spread like a caul over whomever he was with at the time the urgency was upon him, that had co-opted Mimi into the mutual invention of their love. For she was sure now that that was what had happened: they had made up love in the making of love. Inventing intensity was Jack's habitual way of progressing through life, but he spotted something in her for what it was, and she was whirled into his love project, like a bobbin driven by an electric motor. Some hungry hole in Jack demanded to be fed with excitement and gratification. When there was an emotional lull in his life, he filled the void with an invented titillation. Even when the gratification was available he would top himself up to enhance the excitement which was, perhaps, never quite exciting enough. Her own vacancy was of a different nature. A cultivated void that required silence and inactivity to satisfy its emptiness. Yet a hole is a hole, and its essential nature is that it is available to be filled. Whether she believed she wanted it or not, Jack's speed and energy had poured into Mimi who had, up to then, thought herself well protected against invasion.

Love was not Mimi's subject. Never having learned it at her mother's knee, she grew up without placing it at the centre of her life. Without seeing the need for it to be at the centre. A life without love did not seem to her to be a life that was by definition bereft. For one thing, she did not feel bereft. Indeed, when she looked around during her adolescence and early twenties, the most bereft looked like those for whom a life without love was meaningless. She had considered the issue. Was it better to have love, or think you had it, and then lose it? Perhaps regular failure interwoven with bursts of apparent success was better than counting love out of life altogether. It was reasonable to suppose that most people, at this time, in this part of the world, thought so. Still, Mimi did not. Better seemed to mean better than alone, and Mimi did not mind being alone. She acknowledged that it may have been a matter of contingency. Love, as it is generally understood, had not come along, and like the cloth she cut into individual patterns for her clients, her life had acquired a particular shape. But love-as-it-is-understood was at the core of the issue. Mimi did not understand, and had never understood, love. Perhaps the absence of it in an obvious, early way had caused her to make impossible demands of it. Demands which, in their nature, could never be lived up to. Like God, if it was to exist, love had to be perfect and without flaw, and since there was no evidence that it was, and plentiful indications that it wasn't, she dismissed it, like God, as a comforting fantasy she didn't have to have. Once she had done that – placed love in the realm of myth and fairy-tale – it became perfectly possible to have relationships of various kinds without weighing them down, drowning them in impossible expectation. Was this really a loss, a depletion of her life, or simply a different kind of life from that which others sought? Friendship and passion were quite real and achievable, though in Mimi's experience, mutually exclusive. And when friendship wore out and passion faded, it was sad, but not tragic, for nothing eternal had been found wanting, nothing real had been revealed as imaginary. People grew away from each other, as lovers, as friends, and it was no more tragic that the Second Law of Thermodynamics. It was not unreasonable to feel a gentle melancholy in the face of the immutable increase of entropy, but it was not something to be surprised and disappointed about. False disapppointment seemed to Mimi to lie at the heart of discontent.

Mimi was not merely a passive victim of Jack's flooding force. Though her attraction to it was initially unwilled, her admittance of Jack into her life had something considered about it. When she thought about the mismatch between them and the increasing passion they whipped up in each other, she found, apart from the sexual pleasure which she had no trouble justifying, a more earnest purpose for allowing it to continue. How could she know for sure that her need for silence and solitude was real and not simply an evasion of life, unless she permitted Jack to test it? She thought in the interests of objective truth, as well as naked lust, that she should allow herself to be caught up in Jack's whirlwind. Perhaps her desire for silence was a mere conceit. A story she told herself. In the manner of a scientific investigator she should see what happened when she told herself a different story.

Jack and Mimi had met three years before when his wife suggested Jack try her dressmaker for a suit. He had been resistant, or so he told Mimi.

'I don't want a frock. I need a tailor not a dressmaker.'

Tricia had jeered.

'Just go and see her stuff. She makes clothes for little boys, too.'

'I'm a *big* boy, a big, big, big boy,' Jack growled, beating his chest gorilla-style. Jack told Mimi that he seemed to remember he and Tricia had made love after that.

Mimi's flat was in a basement reached separately from the rest of the house by stairs descending below the pavement. Inside was the silence and Mimi, both of which in the first few moments he had thought dull. Mimi wore a long black skirt and grey shirt hanging loosely outside. The outfit was shape-concealing, utterly unadorned; as plain as some of the plainest clothes she had made for Tricia, which Jack found too simple and unsexy, though he recognized that the taste was impeccable. Mimi's shoulder-length black hair fell straight to a severe and blunt edge, with no fringe to soften her high rounded forehead and peaked features. She was in her mid-forties, too skinny, her face gaunt and devoid of make-up; there was nothing in the slightest way provocative about her, and Jack liked nothing more than to be provoked by women. She was, he later told her, altogether too stark for his taste and he dismissed her immediately as a potential mistress.

The feeling was mutual. Mimi found very little in the immediate Jack who came through her door that she wanted. He was too big, too brash, entering the flat like a blustery wind through a broken pane of glass. Though his black eye patch was interesting, she found his over-long, flopping, dirty blonde hair too contrived, his eagerness to make his presence felt too invasive. Though she was not looking for a lover, being in a satisfactory and unthreatening relationship already, there was still an automatic assessment of any new man. Would she want to if she wanted to? She decided that if she had been looking for more than a client, she would not look to Jack. Not her type.

Not that he was exactly looking for another woman in his life. It was already complicated enough. He had at that time three or four women on the go – all married and safely unavailable for more than sex – apart from Tricia. He had stopped being faithful to Tricia a year to the day after they married. A kind of anniversary present to himself, he explained to Mimi. Somehow the regular women had accumulated into a weekly routine, though there were others from time to time, women he met in the course of a working day. (A rep from a photocopier company had come to give him a quote at the office when his partner and the secretary were at lunch. He and the rep were fumbling with her under-things in the lavatory within minutes of her giving him a price. She went away happy, even though he decided against upgrading his photocopier.) He saw each of the regular women once a week or so, and between their commitments and his, their meetings required all his considerable organizational talent. But he was prepared to put up with the difficulty since his sexual adventuring made him feel unfettered, though he loved Tricia and had no plans to leave her. Even so, with all the complications, he found himself assessing any women he came across; it was instinctive to consider every woman he met as a potential fuck. It was a fast and immediate decision; how she looked, how she looked at him, yes, no. Mimi hadn't fit the bill at all. Not exciting, not provocative. She looked at him with indifferent, uninviting eyes.

But gradually as they discussed his ideas for a suit, he noticed the silence and how it originated from Mimi herself, radiating out from her centre to fill all the space around her. She was calm, unhurried, asking him practical questions about style and fabric, but contained. So he said. By not demanding any attention for herself – there was not the slightest hint of flirtation – she became an object of curiosity to Jack. Her very refusal to be seductive became interesting and gradually seductive itself. He sensed her interest in making clothes was professional but not passionate, as if there was something other than dressmaking that held her attention even while she spoke to him about his suit. Tricia had said she lived alone, so it was not a husband or children who lurked behind her. The word that came to mind was serenity, not a word that often came to Jack's mind.

'Do you work at home?' he asked.

She showed him into the large back room where she made her clothes. In spite of all the bolts and swatches of fabric lying about, the two half-dressed headless dummies, the sewing-machine and the unfinished garments draped over the arms of chairs and hanging from the picture-rail, the room had a peculiar sense of orderliness about it. It wasn't tidy, but the untidiness seemed patterned, or, at least, purposeful. Two glass doors opened on to a small garden area that was crammed full of green foliage which seemed to press itself towards the room. Although it was summer, there were no flowers, just a multitude of leaf shapes and variations on the colour green. It made Jack smile.

'It's lovely here. Very peaceful.'

'It suits,' she said.

'Doesn't it get dull working alone?'

Mimi shook her head and smiled slightly.

'That's why I do it. I like making clothes and I like being alone.'

She led him out of the room.

'All the time?' he asked as they returned to the living room, and realized he was interested in her after all.

'What do you do?' she asked.

'Ideas. I run a small publishing outfit. Phone calls all the time, people, meetings, offices. I'm a very busy fellow.'

'People like that,' Mimi said, showing not the slightest sign of meeting his developing interest in her head on.

'It's very peaceful here.'

'It's what I like. Not everyone's cup of tea. No reason why it should be.'

'It must be addictive.'

'Yes,' Mimi nodded. 'That's exactly what it is. Sometimes I get quite annoyed when people come for fittings. Then I remember that they're paying my bills. So, the suit?'

'Yes. Yes, I liked your idea. The black.'

'I'll take your measurements.'

Jack stood crucified for several moments while she ran a tape across, down and around various parts of his body, gauging the length of his arms and legs, the width of his back, the circumference of his waist and chest.

'Turn-ups?' she queried.

'Turn-ups,' he nodded. 'If you think they're a good idea.'

'Why not?' she smiled and dropped to her knees in front of him to measure the distance between his instep and ankle.

Jack looked down at her and discovered that he wanted to see her in that position minus the shirt and skirt. He wanted very much to see her breasts which he judged to be small but firm beneath their prim cotton covering. Her thinness no longer troubled him. He imagined an interesting mixture of pain and pleasure as the sharp bones of her hips dug further and further into the top of his thighs. He thought of placing his hand against the back of her head while she kneeled in front of him, and stroking her sleek hair, of cupping the palm of his hand around her head and encouraging her forward, in towards him, and with the other hand unzipping his trousers, when he realized he was still standing with his arms spread-eagled at shoulder height.

'Can I put my arms down now?'

She didn't look up at him, continuing to measure around his ankles.

'Best keep them where they are for the moment,' she said.

This was a woman to be left alone, Jack thought, or given time. He still had not made up his mind about her. At any rate, she was a different proposition from the photocopier rep.

'When's the first fitting?' he asked.

Two weeks later she phoned to tell him he could come for a fitting. Mimi had been much in his thoughts in the interim. He recollected her in her pool of silence in the basement flat, and found himself wanting whatever it was she created around her. It was something Jack had never tried, never been able to try, and he began to want it for himself. His life had been quite different. He had, for as long as he could remember, striven, using every ounce of energy he had to get out and up. To get somewhere. Stillness was outside his experience, it looked brand new to him. It came to seem as if Mimi had a secret which he might receive if he could be close enough to her, if he could share, daily, nightly in it. It had a power which intrigued him, and which he suspected he could make great use of. It was an entirely other way, and he found himself wanting it greedily and with increasing passion.

He arranged the fitting for the following evening, saying he was too busy to come during the day and turned up with two bottles of wine. Mimi raised her eyebrows slightly when he handed them to her. After the fitting he asked for a corkscrew.

Mimi sat on her sofa in the same long black skirt, though, this time, with a white shirt on top, her legs curled under her, sipping the wine. Her willingness to turn the fitting into a social occasion encouraged Jack, but it was the only visible encouragement she offered. Jack filled Mimi's silence with his words. He talked about himself, wanting her to know about him, and that he was not just another fast whizzkid. He had come from somewhere real and made himself into something, and he was not finished. He wanted her to know how much he had made of himself and how much more there was left of him; his quirkiness and cleverness, and the unexpected places in him that needed to meet their match in order to evolve. He wanted her to feel he was different. He watched her carefully as he spoke, trying to work out if he was lighting any spark of interest. He talked into the space she created by her silence, radiating energy about the room as she radiated stillness, while she sat quietly, smiling and nodding, but looking vaguely anxious, a little alarmed, like a gazelle getting wind of something lurking in the bushes. He found himself feeling too large, too loud, and tried to quell his size and suppress his vigour, not wanting to frighten her off. It wasn't easy, even a small portion of his forcefulness made jagged holes in the quietness of the room and its occupant.

He told her about his youth in Sheffield and his father who worked in a steel foundry, like his brother did, like he was supposed to.

'I was built for it. No one in my family thought much of education. It wasn't manly. There wasn't any use for it. Cleverness didn't put food on the table, not as far as they were concerned, and reading books was for women, though they didn't in my family. It would have been all right if I'd been small and weakly. They'd have dismissed me as fit for nothing else, but I grew big and strong, in spite of my wavy hair and pretty blue eyes, and looked like one of them. My dad used to show me off to his mates in the pub. "He'll be taller than me." So when I took to booklearning he felt betrayed. I'd let him down. I could have been a man, but chose not to be. That was how he saw it.'

'Why did you take an interest in books?'

'A teacher. The classic thing. Someone at school seeing something and making you the offer of another life. There was a little more to it, though. She was a woman in her thirties, not married – one of those dedicated types who wanted to bring culture to the working classes. A dried-up old spinster, my dad called her when he caught me in dark corners reading books she'd lent me. But he was wrong, she wasn't dried up at all.'

'You became lovers?'

'From the age of fourteen until I left for university, although by then, it had become a bit one-sided.'

'So she taught you everything you know?' Mimi smiled.

'The physical side of it was more of a mutual investigation. She wasn't dried-up – the juices were there and ready to run – but she was a spinster. I was her first lover since her fiancé had been killed just before the end of the war. They'd only had sex the once – she'd only had sex the once – the last time he was on leave. He persuaded her he might not come back, and he was right. She went to teacher-training college after that and devoted herself to education. She knew less about sex than I did, I think. But we both learned fast.'

'What was her name?'

'Julia. She was no beauty. A skinny, plain-looking woman, but she had passion. I couldn't understand how she'd managed to suppress it all the years between the dead boyfriend and me coming along.'

'And after you went to university?'

'It petered out. We kept in touch, and at first I went to see her during the vacations. But I'd discovered a new world – not just girls, everything new. I stopped going back to Sheffield and started to travel during the vacations, and I didn't keep up the letters. She knew it had to end. She taught me so that I'd get away from my background, and she was part of it. She never complained. She went on teaching. Once or twice we bumped into each other when I was still going home for Christmas. She'd aged, of course. It was as if we were just an old teacher and her pupil meeting on the street. I tried to be friendlier than that, but she edged away and refused anything more intimate than a handshake when I'd finished telling how I was getting on.'

'Sad. Cruel, even.'

Jack was jarred by Mimi's sentimentality. Until then he had been pleased to discover himself talking to someone who, for all her quietness, understood, like himself, the realities of life, and seemed to acknowledge the overall irony – the way things were – with a small smile and let it go. He had spoken to her wryly, as an equal. He had supposed her to be that from the inside. There was a rush of disappointment, as he realized how much she had excited him without even knowing it himself. His expectation that Mimi was outside the social mimsery was dashed.

'It'd have been sadder for her if she'd found no one,' he said briskly.

Mimi laughed, sharp and harsh.

'How sentimental you are,' she said with an amused look. 'Another one with such a high regard for love that the idea of anyone doing very nicely without it is incomprehensible.'

Jack's faith in Mimi recovered, though he felt now that it was he who had fallen from grace in her eyes. He was not used to such a feeling and he didn't like it. He fought back.

'I wasn't talking about love, I was talking about fucking. I think it's better to have fucked and lost than never to have fucked at all. Is that what you mean by sentimental?'

'Certainly. Do you think people can't be sentimental about fucking? Did Julia take other schoolboy lovers after you?'

'No,' Jack was definite.

'How do you know if you didn't keep in touch?'

It was unthinkable.

'She wouldn't have.'

Mimi smiled and shrugged. Jack had not been redeemed. He

sensed an amused contempt for him which irritated him. He recognized it clearly and uncomfortably; it was what he usually felt for other people. She had smiled and left the matter at that, as if it was still a question hanging in the air that he had failed to answer properly. He knew Julia. Mimi was in no position to have that faintly superior look on her face.

'What about you?' Jack asked, moving the burden of conversation on to her life.

'I've had sex more than once,' she said.

'Are you going to have sex with me?' Jack asked, deciding it was time to get her off-centre and choosing his usual way of achieving it.

'You're married,' she said, without a flicker of disturbance.

'Yes.'

'Is it a good marriage?'

'Yes.'

'Then perhaps we will have sex. Let's get the suit finished first.'

'What if I'd said I was unhappily married?' he asked, a little confused himself.

'I try not to have relationships with unhappily married men. People who are in bad marriages sometimes get their emotional needs in a muddle.'

'You're never in a muddle, then?'

'Often, but I try not to be in company.'

The fitting was over. Jack left with all sorts of unspoken promises ringing in his ear, yet also with the feeling that he was in pursuit of a reluctant quarry.

They had shared those early impressions of each other with each other while they were at the height of their passion. The initial reluctance, the misreading, the wrong-footing of both of them somehow added to the momentousness of their passion. When he told her of his many mistresses, his deception of his wife, his incapacity for fidelity, it was with the explicit purpose of describing how utterly changed a creature he was with her. Their love, once it was up and running, was to be unlike anything either of them had experienced before. It was to negate all their previous tendencies because this was, for both of them, *the* love. The one that put everything else into perspective. 'Ahh, that was why I was incapable of staying true to a woman for very long: I hadn't yet met you.' This thing of theirs was different, and it could never flag, because its very nature was other. 'I could never want anyone but you. I never will.'

Mimi was less convinced, or possessed less talent for conviction.

'Never?' she said, believing, at least, that currently he didn't want anyone else.

'Never,' Jack would insist. 'You are it.'

Mimi couldn't imagine wanting anyone else. But she could imagine that she might be wrong. She would make a leap in time and see herself turn back to the present with a knowing smile. It was not a picture she indulged, but it was there. When she asked him if he ever had the same picture, Jack said she didn't love him as much as he loved her.

Sometimes Mimi thought that that was simply true, though their lust was equal. But she came to understand that Jack did not make imaginative leaps into the future, or rather, his imagined future was little more than the vision of his present thoughts come true, a land not so much of wish-fulfilment as presumption. The great difference between them apart from their radically different energy levels (a physical thing surely) was that it was Jack who had done the leaving in his early life – away from home and family – while for Mimi the leaving had been on the part of others, so that she knew, as Jack seemed not to know, the future could not be simply what one made up for oneself in the present, but depended to some unknown extent on the behaviour of others. It made the future far less knowable, and the present far less of a reliable guide to what might happen. Jack, on the other hand, had maintained his belief in his control of events. Curiously, for all the discomfort of her own position, she did not envy Jack his assurance about the future, feeling that, in the long run, her uncertainty painted the more accurate picture of events. It seemed that, in this case at least, she had been proven right. But then Jack, having been wrong about the forever of their love, would not be dismayed. When his future came and turned out to be different from his projections, he simply transformed it into the current present, which provided a brand new, certain future to look forward to. Mimi had smelled it on his fingers the previous night.

Mimi glanced at the clock. It was eleven-fifteen. I could get up, she thought, but didn't. There was no impulse to start the day. She played her consciousness like a game. Mimi allowed the sexually tinged mist of sleep to creep up on her while seemingly preoccupied with her thoughts. Slumber, in its physical form, sneaked through her veins and arteries, camouflaged among the white and red blood cells making their dogged ways towards her heart. Like a latter-day Mistress Quickly tracking the venous path of death through Sir John Falstaff's nether regions, beginning at the extremities and moving upwards to strike its final blow at the heart, Mimi surreptitiously followed the less tragic ascent of sleep through her own body. Death and sleep took the same route; they were, after all, related. Mimi kept a covert inner eye on sleep's progress, permitting it to run almost to its full extent, to the point where she could savour her inability to keep the narrative of her thoughts running connectedly on, and relish the misty other place which hazed reality before the fall into full and blank unconsciousness. The great skill was to judge the moment perfectly, to achieve the odd, remarkably delicious pleasure of half-sleep without allowing it to slip away from her control. At the precise moment of the disappearance of the world, she sprung her surprise on herself and brought her mind back to a more or less everyday alertness.

Mimi much preferred to play solitaire in this way. She knew from long ago that in the end the games people played with each other were threats. The game seemed all the better this morning for the leisurely sense she had of the day getting on quite nicely by itself without demanding her attention. As she alternated curious torpid states of mind with clearer thoughts, her lazy, hazy morning continued. Why shouldn't it, she told herself. Everyone was entitled to a long lie-in every now and again. Hers was going to be very long indeed.

Even so, with all her skill at tracking and holding back sleep, there were periods when sleep overtook her, though they were so brief that she would have denied them if anyone had been there to point them out. Her control was rather less than she supposed, and sleep rather subtler than she gave it credit for. Given her habit of dreamlessness, or her inability to remember what dreams she may have had, it was difficult for her to pinpoint her dips into unconsciousness.

Mr Abrahams was almost a rabbi. Being a young man – he was in his mid-twenties – he was full enough of energy and enthusiasm to take the trouble to make himself available to the Jewish children in Miriam's primary school. There were only four of them, but Mr Abrahams took them off to a small classroom each Wednesday at the end of school and attempted to teach them Hebrew. Miriam went along, partly to put off for a while going home to the lamenting mother, and partly because, after the St Martin's incident, learning Hebrew seemed very slightly to enlarge the solid ground beneath her feet.

'Call me Leonard,' Mr Abrahams announced at the first lesson. He was a liberal educator and felt he would get the best from his four charges if they distinguished him from their everyday teachers. Miriam, however, refused to call him anything but Mr Abrahams. This was not because of any innate respect Miriam had for her elders and betters, but because she thought 'Leonard' was a ridiculous and embarrassing name and couldn't bring herself to say it. That was the reason originally, though, of course, names, even the strangest and silliest, get attached to the people they belong to after a while, and always become sayable in time. Even when 'Leonard' had become ordinary enough with use by the other members of the class, she continued to refuse to call him anything other than Mr Abrahams, mostly because she had begun by refusing, and to change her mind seemed to be a climb down from somewhere, even though she knew no very great principle was involved.

But there was something else. Mr Abrahams badly wanted her to call him by his first name. The more she didn't, the badder he wanted it, and the badder he wanted it, the more she didn't want to give him what he wanted. He didn't say anything particularly, but Miriam could tell. And she noticed how he glanced at her frequently during the class, more than the others. It became almost a game, calling him Mr Abrahams, and watching the flicker of disappointment cross his face. The game continued when he asked her questions and, knowing the answer, she would shrug.

'Don't know.'

'Yes, you do. I know you know,' he'd insist, something intense in his eyes and voice. For some reason it was terribly important to him that she knew the answers.

'No, Mr Abrahams, really I don't,' she'd tell him with a little smile at his raised, disbelieving eyebrows.

But at the end of the lesson, as she disappeared through the door, she'd turn and whisper the answer towards his desk. Mr Abrahams would burst out laughing, almost in relief.

'You're a minx,' he'd say, shaking his head and finger at her, his eyes turning oddly soft.

She thought of it as teasing. He was easy to tease, like a kitten wanting to play a game, not wanting to catch the wriggling string too soon, or the game would be over. There was something in Mr Abrahams' eyes that delighted in her making fun of him, and seemed to ask for more. But when his silent request was most intensely visible, Miriam would shut down and become a quiet, ordinary pupil, answering questions accurately and refusing to play the game. A funny feeling, some kind of unease, would come over her, and she became polite and distant.

Mr Abrahams started to make visits to her home, hearing that the family was in difficulty, and taking his parochial role seriously. Miriam's mother welcomed him into her world of woe. He sat and listened to her complaints, her desolation and destitution, and shook his head in shock and sympathy that a man, a *Jewish* man, should have left his family in such a way. He found a Jewish fund to help out a little with the financial problems. He agreed with Leah that she had had a most unfortunate and terrible life, and suffered from a miserable marriage to a man whose behaviour was a shame to Judaism. Mr Abrahams wanted to try and ease the burden on her, he explained, and in pursuit of this goal, he arranged for Leah to have a break from looking after Miriam during the next school holidays. He understood how difficult it was having a young child around all the time when she had so many worries.

That first time Miriam stayed with a family in Golders Green. They were well-intentioned people, who wanted to help a disadvantaged Jewish child, but for Miriam it was difficult. It was hard to know, when living in the house of strangers, how to behave, to what extent she should keep out of the family's way, how much she should try to join in. She didn't want to join in, but sometimes she thought she ought to, to show gratitude for their kindness, and sometimes she thought she shouldn't for exactly the same reason.

They were very orthodox, and seemed to Miriam constantly to be going to synagogue. They took her along with them, and separated at the entrance, the father and sons going one way, she and Ruth and Ruth's mother going the other, to the women's section. Ruth tried to help Miriam with the prayers, but found it astonishing that she, a Jewish girl like herself, should know so little about her own religion. Miriam, for her part, tried, thinking it was the least she could do, and somehow wanting to apologize to God for her mother's secret trips to church, but the Jewish prayers remained deeply mysterious, and worse, she had terrible problems with ceremony. She wanted to laugh at all the men downstairs, dipping their upper bodies to and fro as they muttered prayers, like reciting a shopping list in a foreign language, and she thought the winding and unwinding of the little black box with long leather ties around their arms very peculiar. She couldn't see what that had to do with God, though Ruth explained it was symbolic of how they would always keep God's words close to their hearts and minds. On Fridays, the mother lit the *shabbos* candles and, placing her hands on top of their heads, blessed all the children in front of them, including Miriam, who liked the idea of being blessed, but couldn't work out why this woman who was generally up to her elbows in baking and singeing chickens could do such a solemn task. It was also another ritual during which she had to choke back her giggles of embarrassment. She bit the insides of her cheeks until they bled to keep control. And, of course, on Friday nights, she always forgot she was not supposed to switch on the lights. When she did, often very late to go to the bathroom, the whole family, mother, father, two brothers and sister would run out of their rooms in alarm.

'Who did that?' they would shriek frantically to each other, as if God would only give them a few seconds to find the culprit. Miriam always owned up, and they told her and told her, though not too unkindly, about the Sabbath and not doing any work. But there was some relief, Miriam thought, that it was not one of them who had broken the Lord's commandments. Miriam was an outsider, whose guilt did not devolve on the family who had temporarily taken her in.

After that, Mr Abrahams arranged for her to stay with two or three other families at half-terms and holidays, and he would drive her there and pick her up to take her back to her mother. She didn't like it much, staying with strangers and being a charity case. Everyone treated her well, and tried to be tactful, even when at Passover one family bought her a new pair of shoes, saying it was traditional and everyone had to have something new at *Pesach*. But why else was she being shipped off to people she'd never met, if she wasn't a charity case? She told her mother she didn't want to go on these 'holidays' any more, but Leah began to shout, telling her not to be so bloody ungrateful. There was Mr Abrahams putting himself out for them, Leah didn't know what she'd do without him; thank God, at last, someone was taking an interest in them, and Miriam, having no consideration for her mother's problems, was a thankless little cow.

During the long summer holiday, Miriam stayed with three

families, to spread the burden. The last was Mr Abraham's own sister, Myra, who lived in Luton with her rabbi husband and their baby son. Mr Abrahams was on holiday himself and taking it with his sister too, partly, he said, so that he would be able to give Miriam special tuition in Hebrew and Jewish history. One night, she woke the household, screaming her way out of one of her nebulous and terrifying nightmares. Myra rushed in to the spare room to find the ten-year-old drenched and wild-eyed with terror, still half in her fearsome dream. She made the child some cocoa and then sat with her, asking Miriam what she had been dreaming about, but Miriam wouldn't or couldn't say and just shivered.

'What's this?' Myra asked, taking a book from the tangle of covers where it had lain since Miriam had fallen asleep with it in her hand. Miriam was sniffing her way back to the real world and beginning to find the cocoa and the woman sitting on the edge of her bed comforting.

The book was *The Scourge of the Swastika* by Lord Russell of Liverpool. Its title was in screaming red print, and the book was open half-way through at a hazy photograph of a long line of women of about Myra's age, standing in the open air, all of them completely naked, while uniformed men brandishing sticks looked directly at them. The women were huddled over, using their hands to try to cover their breasts and private parts. They looked cold in the wintry scene, but though you couldn't see their eyes, their distress at their nakedness was clear, as they stood incongruously in a queue seeming to wait for instructions. The men in uniform stared at the women, one or two with slight smiles on their faces, others with cold-eyed disgust.

'Where did you get this?' Myra said, frowning and closing the book.

'Mr Abrahams gave it to me.'

'He had no business giving you a book like this,' Myra said. 'It's not for a child.'

'He said I should see what happened to our people. He said it really happened. Myra,' Miriam whispered, as the ghost of her dream came back to her, 'I don't want to be Jewish.'

'That's all over now,' Myra said, stroking Miriam's hair. 'It happened far away, and it's over. Nothing like that could happen again. And it wouldn't happen here, in England. You don't need to read any more of this.'

Myra took the book away with her when she left, after making sure that Miriam had settled to a peaceful sleep.

Miriam liked Myra, who taught her how to iron shirt collars – you started from the middle of the collar and worked out to either end, that way the fabric wouldn't get ruched up at the centre. There were also cooking lessons, and learning how to change the baby's nappy. Little Benjamin was the first baby Miriam had ever had anything to do with. Myra trusted her to hold him and showed her how to bathe him in the small kidney-shaped basin with its own special foldaway stand.

On the day before Miriam was due to leave, Myra suggested an outing to the town centre, but Mr Abrahams, who had come for the day and was staying the night so he could take Miriam home in the morning, vetoed the idea.

'Miriam and I will do a little work. A quiet day won't hurt.'

Myra left, saying she and the baby would be back by teatime.

'Well, what shall we do today?' Mr Abrahams said. 'I've had a severe telling-off from Myra about the book I gave you. We're not allowed to talk about that.'

He invited Miriam to chuckle with him, but she turned on the television. The Olympics were on; people were running, jumping and throwing themselves and javelins through space. Miriam sat in the armchair. Mr Abrahams pulled a wooden chair from the dining table and sat on it next to Miriam.

'Sport,' he said, contemptuously. 'People running fast and getting nowhere.'

'I like it,' Miriam said, though she didn't. She wished she had gone with Myra, not happy at being alone all day with Mr Abrahams. She didn't feel like the usual bantering, in fact she wished he would be quiet so she could pretend he wasn't there.

'Are you in a bit of a mood today?' he asked, pulling his chair closer to hers.

'No,' she said, moodily.

'Well, you're not very friendly, are you? Who's winning?'

'The one in front,' Miriam said, and then regretted it, hearing Mr Abrahams laugh.

'That's better. But how do you know it's not a losing race? They have them, you know – the last man wins – sometimes when they think they can get away with it, they run backwards – of course, you can't tell, they mark time for a while, just pumping their legs up and down and it makes your brain think they're moving forward, but really all the time they're deceiving you and . . .'

He went on and on, babbling nonsense and gasping for breath instead of pausing. While he spoke, he moved his chair right up against Miriam's until he was close enough to lay an arm across the top of her chair, just inches from the back of her neck. It was the fear in his voice which made Miriam so nervous. His jabbering was almost as if he were trying to distract himself as well as her from his increasing movements towards her. Miriam really didn't know what was happening, but there was a bad feeling, a foreboding in the pit of her stomach. The skin on the back of her neck prickled at the closeness of his arm behind her. Then the arm slipped gently down the back of the chair to rest on her shoulders, as if it had got there by accident. Miriam jumped away out of the chair. She wanted to say stop it, but she imagined him saying, 'Stop what?' and she wouldn't know the answer.

'The picture's too dark,' she said, and crossed the room, sitting in a chair beside the TV set and fiddling with the knobs. The screen immediately snowed, and the picture disappeared. She went on twisting the knobs.

Mr Abrahams dropped vertically off the front of his chair and fell to his knees on the carpet. Miriam gave up her pretence of trying to achieve something with the television knobs, and stared at him.

'What are you doing?' Her voice was a couple of octaves higher than usual.

Mr Abrahams began to crawl on his knees, like a monk

111

approaching an altar, across the living room towards her.

'Please call me Leonard,' he whispered, his register dropping to a husky rasp, just as hers had lifted. 'I want to hear you call me by my name. We're very good friends, aren't we?'

Miriam couldn't say anything at all as she watched him crawl towards her. It seemed to take an incredibly long time, but she was frozen into immobility. *It* was going to happen, whatever *it* was. She was frightened, appalled and embarrassed in equal measure at the sight of Mr Abrahams approaching on his knees. When he arrived, he stopped, his chest against her legs, and looked up into her face. Was this the first time she'd looked down at an adult? Certainly, the angle seemed very unfamiliar. He was still on his knees, his arms hopelessly hanging at his sides, and he remained like that for a moment, somehow dangling there, at her mercy, begging, a supplicant, but a threat, too. He lifted his arms and held his hands parallel to her face, but wide of each cheek, as if waiting for consent to close the distance between his flesh and hers. It was permission he wanted.

'Miriam,' he said, almost choking. She could see tears in his eyes. 'Miriam, I want to kiss you. Can I kiss you? Please. Can I kiss you?'

Miriam, the frozen princess, was awakened by the request for a kiss.

'No!' she screeched, and pushed her bare, bony knees into his chest, unbalancing him, toppling him back on to the carpet enough for her to wriggle herself around his body and bolt from the room. She fled upstairs to the spare bedroom and turned the key in the lock. She sat cross-legged, holding her breath, in the dead centre of the double bed. Mr Abrahams was outside a moment later, banging urgently on the door, appealing to her in a plaintive voice that frayed into panic around its edges.

'Miriam, let me in. Please, let me in. I'm not going to hurt you. I swear. I wouldn't hurt you. I love you.'

Though she was terrified he would break the door down, she tried very hard to pretend he didn't exist. She picked a pile of comics from the floor beside the bed, and made an effort to concentrate wholeheartedly on the exploits of Spiderman and Wonder Woman, though all she was in fact doing was turn the pages. Mr Abrahams' tone changed.

'Miriam, stop this. You misunderstood. You must let me in . . . There's no need to be upset, you didn't understand. Everything's all right. Like always. Talk to me.'

Miriam didn't answer. Mr Abrahams' voice took on a note of simulated calm, though a tremulous sob in his throat belied it.

'All right. If you want to stay in your room this afternoon that's all right. That's perfectly all right. Don't worry, I'll tell Myra you aren't feeling well. I thought this morning you didn't look well. That's why I suggested you stay in. Do you think you've got a temperature? Would you like some hot lemon and honey? You just rest. But will you let me in? I've got to talk to you. Please, Miriam? All right. Listen – can you hear me? – when Myra comes . . . there's no need to tell her. To say anything. I mean, nothing happened. Nothing was going to happen. Just say you're not feeling well. You've got a touch of 'flu, I think. That's it, you've probably got the 'flu, it's going round . . . But please . . . don't say anything. Don't imagine things.'

Eventually, his voice trailed away into something between a groan and a whimper, and he went downstairs. Miriam continued to turn the pages of her comics until Myra and the baby came home. After a few minutes there was a knock at the door. Miriam opened it, and let Myra put a concerned hand on her forehead.

'Leonard's right, you *are* a bit warm. Would you like me to bring you supper up here? You stay in bed, and we'll wrap you up nice and warm for the drive back to London tomorrow.'

Miriam had not forgotten that the next morning Mr Abrahams would be driving her back to London in his little Mini. Just the two of them. She hardly slept that night.

In the morning there was nothing more than a grunted greeting at breakfast, after which Mr Abrahams was silent and kept his head down reading the paper from cover to cover. Miriam would rather have walked back to London than sit beside Mr Abrahams in the small car, so much smaller than the room he had crossed on his knees the previous day, and with no place to run to. But she dared not mention to Myra what had happened.

They proceeded along the motorway in silence, Mr Abrahams looking ahead at the road, Miriam staring fixedly out of her side window, until they were half-way back to London. Suddenly, although they'd passed a service station just five minutes before, Miriam felt the car slowing down, and a moment later, still without a word, Mr Abrahams steered into an empty lay-by. He stopped and switched off the ignition. There was very little traffic on the road. The quiet was emphasized by the sudden swish of a car passing at speed, as they sat, each staring straight ahead out through their side of the windscreen.

Now, it's going to happen, Miriam thought, barely breathing, wanting to swallow but not daring to make any kind of noise. What was going to happen was all the more dreadful for being unknown. From the corner of her eye she kept Mr Abrahams' hands on the steering wheel in view, until finally, after several deep breaths, when he seemed as if he might begin to talk but didn't, he turned towards her.

'Miriam,' he said in a voice that was deeply serious and resonated with authority. 'I want to ask you something.'

He paused. Miriam waited, watching his hands which had not moved but seemed to have become clawlike and white at the knuckles with clutching the wheel. She stealthily moved one of hers nearer to the latch that opened her door.

'I just want to say this. I very much hope that what . . . happened yesterday . . . what occurred between us . . . I just want to say that I hope it hasn't in any way changed your feelings towards our religion.'

Miriam suppressed the desire to answer: 'Nothing happened. What religion? What yesterday?' and shook her head vigorously in an access of relief. Like Joan of Arc in one of the comics she'd read, Miriam realized she could be reprieved if she just gave him the answer he wanted, though what religion had to do with yesterday was beyond her comprehension. Unlike Joan of Arc, she only wanted not to burn.

114

'No. Oh no. I like our religion. It's the best one.'

'You won't stop going to *schule*?'

'No. No. I won't. I mean, I will – be going to *schule* regularly. As often as I can. I like going to *schule*.'

Mr Abrahams nodded his relief.

'And better not say anything to your mother. She wouldn't understand.'

'No. Can we go on now, please?'

He nodded again before turning on the ignition. They continued the rest of the drive back to London in silence.

Miriam had lied. She never did go to *schule* again, although her religious lapse was probably not the result of Mr Abrahams crawling across the room to her on his knees. She still didn't see what religion had to do with it. She probably wouldn't have gone to synagogue anyway, and if she had kept away to avoid meeting Mr Abrahams, it wouldn't have worked. He still turned up and drank tea with Leah, who seemed to guess nothing, although Miriam made herself scarce whenever she knew he was expected. Quite often, though, he was there when she got back from school, and she hated the way he looked at her as she greeted him politely. As if there was something between them. A secret they shared that his eyes silently warned her was for them alone. But she knew he was right about not telling her mother. Miriam knew it *was* her fault, that she'd sort of known something was going on almost from the beginning, although she didn't know exactly what, and she had let it go on until what nearly happened nearly happened. Her mother would kill her and then die of shame if she found out.

But she also badly didn't want to keep finding Mr Abrahams in the flat. She hated coming in and seeing him sitting there. Finally, when Miriam's mother said she was going to ask him about the coming half-term, to see if there was somewhere Miriam could go for a nice break, she decided which was the worse alternative: being killed by her mother, or being alone again with Mr Abrahams.

Leah was standing with her back to Miriam, which helped her to screw up the courage to blurt out what had happened in Luton.

'He tried to kiss me.'

She tensed herself for the reaction. Her mother would ask 'Who tried to kiss you?' Miriam would explain what happened. Then there would be screaming and shouting, and in all likelihood, her mother would hit her, but that, and the long aftermath of recrimination, would be better than being whisked off again by Mr Abrahams.

There was a moment's silence before Leah turned towards her daughter. Miriam imagined she was working up to her explosion, summoning the extra energy needed. But when her mother eventually turned around there was a smile on her face.

'He'll be a proper rabbi in a year or so,' she said, seeming to talk to herself. 'And you'll be old enough to get married in three or four years' time. You'd be amazed at how quickly the years pass. It would be something – to be a rabbi's wife,' she told her daughter dreamily.

Although Miriam couldn't realize it at the time, Leah had reverted to the old ways. There was nothing strange in the *shtetl* about an eligible young man with good prospects casting his eye around and finding a promising young girl to whom he could become betrothed. A man with prospects looked at a ten-year-old, and saw qualities that suited, to be moulded and refined into the makings of a good wife.

'I could tell from the way he looked at you that he felt something,' Miriam's mother, almost a rabbi's mother-in-law, said. 'You just play your cards right, and you could have a very nice marriage. Try and be a little more friendly. You've been very sulky around him lately.'

Luckily for Miriam, Mr Abrahams disappointed Leah soon after that, when he and the fund for distressed Jewish families disappeared from their lives. When she phoned to find out where he was, it seemed he'd suddenly decided to continue his training in the north of England, where he now planned to settle.

'Men,' Leah spat. 'You can't trust any of them. And don't talk to me about the Jews, they're as bad as all the rest.'

It seemed that Mr Abrahams had had a negative effect on

Leah's faith in her religion, if not her daughter's. Not long after her first visit to St Martin's-in-the-Fields, a book appeared by Leah's bedside. It was a large book, full of coloured drawings and big print, designed for children. It was called *Tales of the New Testament*.

Mimi jerked back into consciousness. It was still only eleven-forty-five. The fact that Jack would not be coming back after work made time seem luxuriously endless today. She threw back the duvet and lay for a moment giving herself the opportunity to want to get up. She didn't. She gave the duvet a bit of a shake and let it drop back around her.

She had known that Jack was being unfaithful to her, though she couldn't tell if he was having an affair or just screwing around as he had been doing when she first met him. She had no idea when she stopped being the only woman he fucked. Very likely it was the same for her as it had been for Tricia. He had told her all about his infidelity to his wife during their first long vacation together, just before he had moved in with Mimi, though, even then, she had understood Jack's version as the partial account it couldn't help but be.

He had not married Tricia with the intention of being unfaithful to her; on the contrary, he had a passionate commitment to her. In Jack's version, the fact that the occasion of his first infidelity fell on their first anniversary was more a matter of Tricia's treachery than his. When she'd told him she was going away for the weekend to stay with her mother who had been taken ill, he'd shrugged and taken himself off to the pub for some serious solitary drinking. 'Fuck you, too,' he'd thought.

The woman (What was her name? Very likely Jack had never known) had been on the other side of the bar with a man, but by closing time she was standing next to Jack and her companion had left. Jack bought her a couple of drinks and then as the second bell rang he asked her, 'Want to do it?' There was no doubt in his mind what her answer would be. The want-to-do-it question, dormant for a year or more, was a moment of exhilaration, like

117

smashing through a plate glass window and getting out into the air. His body gathered itself together as he spoke it and exhaled a silent roar of affirmation. Fuck *you*! it bellowed back at Tricia who had made herself unavailable to his need. The stale air he left behind him as he popped his question to – whatever her name was – in the bar was the air of his fidelity to his wife. Fuck you, Tricia. Want to do it, Carol (let us say)? One and the same sentence.

Carol, as it happened, had a good body, though he wondered vaguely how clean it was – her hair certainly looked as if it could do with a wash. But Carol could have been a crone for all Jack cared at the moment of his request. What Jack wanted was an unfamiliar fuck and the surge of freedom that would hit him as he expressed himself into her useful and unrecognized body. Fuck you, Tricia; thanks, Whatsyourname.

They shared half a bottle of Scotch back at her place, and Carol served her purpose energetically. She held her drink well, something Jack admired in a woman and required in a man, and when they were finished and Jack gathered enough energy to get himself dressed, she waved him off sleepily without asking when she would see him again. Carol was altogether admirably incurious, a lucky find in an unknown quantity. Of course, she had asked him about the patch over his right eye. He told her he had lost the eye while he was photographing the Afghan war; a stray piece of shrapnel had ended his career with the camera. That story. She was moderately impressed and left it at that. Didn't ask to see behind the patch, which put her in the top one per cent of incurious women. Jack even thought of getting her phone number, but decided not to tempt fate. Seeing more of women who seemed to be prepared to settle for what they were offered had got him into some of his stickiest commitments. He liked to think he'd learned something over the years. In any case, once he'd closed the door behind her, vomited in the road and was driving home, he thought, fuck you, Carol – though with a certain gratitude and even some mild feelings of affection.

Jack, of course, had never been to Afghanistan, or to any other war-torn land, other than that which resided in his own embattled

118

guts. He had lost his right eye a year or so before he married Tricia, at the back of a jazz club in Soho when he and the wife of his best friend had slipped away in the middle of a set. 'Want to do it?' he'd whispered in her ear at the table, as if he was making some point about the music. He followed her out to the lavatories and then through the back door which led to a blind alley where the dustbins and crates of empty bottles were kept. They had never liked each other, which was part of the pleasure of the thing for both of them. The promise of a quick, sordid, rubbish-littered, treacherous fuck sent thrilled shivers through Jack as he watched her raise her tight skirt and pull down her knickers. He saw the look of triumphant contempt on her face and knew, gleefully, that it matched his own expression. He entered her hard, without any attempt at foreplay, and intended to have them both come fast – easy enough, the idea of what they were doing was enough to bring both of them to a climax with a minimum effort. But he hadn't realized how drunk she was. He pushed into her as she half sat, legs wide, on a lidded dustbin which was not full enough, it turned out, to take the pressure of his thrust without moving. It shunted a few inches back along the concrete and with a shriek she lost what balance she had, rolling off it and taking Jack with her, still throbbing inside her. She fell heavily on her back and was winded, but Jack managed to jerk himself out of her in mid-fall and lurched sideways to save himself. He landed, instead of relatively safely on top of her comfortable curves, to one side of her, falling face down on to a crate of empty wine bottles, one of which impaled his right eye.

Luckily, his alcohol intake anaesthetized much of the pain as he lay moaning among the dustbins while his best friend's wife ran to call an ambulance. They couldn't save his eye, and neither the marriage nor the friendship lasted beyond that evening, but it was a memorably raucous event, Jack had thought, almost worth the losses it incurred. In any case, his sight adjusted soon enough, one eye did a remarkable job of pretending to be two, and the piratical patch added to his looks something mysterious and even, when necessary, heroic. It was a talking point, especially at those

119

moments when he wanted to keep the talk to an efficient minimum. Jack's baby face made him look much younger than his thirty-five years, and innocent as the day was long. This had its uses, but the black eye-patch, its diagonal elastic cutting into his curls at the back of his head, added an incongruence his face needed, a darkness that it had lacked. Behind the patch lay the promise of something beyond the cherubic looks that matched his sharp, derisive words. To the observer the lie of his sweet face was undercut by the truth of the implied black hole beneath its covering patch. It functioned almost as an invitation, or perhaps more usefully as a challenge to take the trouble to find out more. With two eyes, Jack's face pulled at the maternal heart-strings and then it was his job to surprise their owner; with one eye the pull and the surprise were there all at once and the owner of the heart-strings was put into a state of uncertainty about what she was getting. The newly built-in uncertainty was an edge over the observing world that Jack fully appreciated.

Mimi hadn't mentioned the eye-patch when they first met. It was her very lack of curiosity that interested him, just as her initial sexual indifference to him sharpened his appetite. True though that was, it was very likely that both these tendencies in her were also responsible for dulling it.

Long before the first year of fidelity was up, Mimi was disappointing him. At the end of one of his midday visits, when he was still with Tricia, they lingered in each other's arms. It was time to get up for a shower. Lunch was almost over.

'Got to go,' he nuzzled into Mimi's ear.

'Mmm, so long as you come back.'

'Always going to come back. I am yours . . .'

'For all lunch times,' Mimi murmured.

'For good. We're going to be together. It's inevitable. I'm not letting this go.'

'My bloke might have something to say about that,' she smiled, putting her arms around him.

'It's over with him, and my wife. This is too important.'

'Does she know?'

120

'Tricia?' He shrugged inside her arms. 'If she doesn't, she doesn't want to. We've got to be together. Properly together.'

'It's so difficult. What if . .. '

Suddenly, Jack became fierce and lifted himself above her, bracing himself on his arms.

'We've got to be together. That's all that matters. It's that simple.'

'Soon,' Mimi said, stroking his hair and trying to soothe the anger away. 'I know. Very soon.'

'When?'

'I don't know.'

'When?'

'Jack . . .'

Mimi was taken with the idea of inevitability. It made life easier. If something was inevitable there was no need to think of the impracticality, all the different undesirabilities, her own ambivalent feelings. But she couldn't quite accept that her and Jack living together *was* inevitable. It wasn't obvious to her as it seemed to be for Jack. In any case, she didn't really think that Jack believed it inevitable. It seemed to her more like a technique he used to get done what he wanted done, to move his life in the direction of his next whim, because it was the movement, not the whim itself, that was essential to him. Mimi's momentum, on the other hand, was inertia. Still, she envied Jack those dives he made into life, and it was part of his attraction that he seemed to be forcing her to jump in with him. Just for a change. She was standing on the edge, knees flexed, ready almost, but still she could not quite jump.

Jack took himself off to the shower. He was angry. He was ready to give up everything. Walk out on Tricia tomorrow and live with Mimi, but she kept putting if off. Not because she didn't want him, but out of anxiety or something like it about breaking up a marriage. But pity didn't help anyone in a situation like this. Husbands and wives always knew, even if they wouldn't admit it to themselves. Letting it go on too long just caused misery for everyone. It was better to be clean, ruthless about it.

There was less pain that way.

Jack felt he had always been let down by women. By their lack of courage, by their inability to commit themselves totally. They let him down by their hesitation. He was glad, suddenly, that he had spent the previous night with an old lover. Mimi's betrayal – slight but telling – had been pre-empted and punished by that first infidelity to his mistress, even though they had been clear that their relationship was not to be exclusive; she was still seeing her Simon, he was married. Their non-exclusivity pact was about their pre-existing relationships, but Jack had taken a broader view the night before, and he had felt slightly guilty about it. Not about faithlessness to his wife, but to his mistress. Now he was glad. It made them even. It was his answer to her resistance to throwing herself into what they both knew was inevitable. He loved her like he had loved no one else, but she let him down by reining in her desire and trying to make it something easy to manage. Real passion was never easy to manage, it required the tearing down of walls, the ripping up of foundations; the rubbling of everything that had been built before so that there was a new world available for the passion to breathe.

Mimi had been reluctant. She knew that her initial opposition to his leaving Tricia and moving in with her had, in his way of thinking, cast the seeds of the death of their love right from the start. Turned it rotten at the heart, so that it had no chance to flourish. Mimi knew he would be seeing it like that, and that she had travelled the same route from his utter devotion to dislike, as Tricia had. Doubtless, while he remembered how he had fallen in love with Mimi, he thought now that he had mistaken the nature of his desire. He had wanted, he would now be telling himself (and his new mistress), her *ambience*; thought he needed it. It had seemed to him to offer a new way of life. He would be wondering now, with a new passion full blown, if he had actually loved Mimi at all. Certainly, with the new woman there was a different feeling altogether. Different from all the previous loves which had come to nothing in the end.

After his shower Jack had returned to Mimi's bedroom.

122

'I want to go away with you. Two weeks. Somewhere in the sun together. The two of us.'

Mimi laughed.

'Jack, how can we?'

'We just do it.'

'And Tricia? And Simon?'

'I've already told her I'm going on holiday for a fortnight.'

'On your own.'

'Yes.'

'And she said?'

'On your own with whom?'

'To which you replied?'

'That it was none of her fucking business. Mimi, I'm serious. I'm booking a flight for us this afternoon. I'll let you know the dates. Tell Simon anything you like. Business. A desperate need for solitude. What does it matter whether he believes you? Tell him you're in love with me. Just tell him. We're going, Mimi. If we don't we're finished. We need time together.'

'You make it sound like an ultimatum.'

Jack shrugged.

'I'm going away for two weeks. If you want to be with me, you can come.'

'And fuck everyone else?'

'And fuck everyone else.'

If there was something monstrous about this way of dealing with the world, there was also something very peaceful.

But Mimi had lost her peace long ago. She had lost it the day Jack arrived with his suitcases, though it wasn't until the following day, a Sunday, that the panic moved in. Two weeks together in the water-colours of the Caribbean (the maps were to extend, after all: the Lilt Guide to Island Hopping) was long enough to make their separation so difficult that Jack moving in became a foregone conclusion. The only question when they returned, was when. Mimi side-stepped it, managing somehow to go blank when he asked. But she didn't say no. Eventually, Jack had said tomorrow.

'Have you told Tricia?'

'I'll tell her in the morning.'

Mimi wandered away. That was all the conversation there was.

The next morning, around eleven-thirty Jack arrived with his necessities. It wasn't until ten-thirty that Mimi had become real enough to push her clothes to one side of the wardrobe and combine the contents of a couple of her drawers. It was around the time that Jack would have been telling Tricia he was off for good. She didn't think about that. Then she sat and read a book in her workroom as if nothing else were happening that day.

She opened the door, and Jack filled the spaces she had made for him without either of them saying a word. They had passed the rest of that first day making love. Underneath the celebration of their unlimited time together, the sex they had with each other, hour after hour, camouflaged the shock of what had been done. Even for Jack the finality of leaving one wife and one life was something. Just for a moment, after the shirts and underpants had been put away they had stood and stared at each other. Now what? Even choosing not to think of the wife who had been left behind with extra space in her wardrobe, there was still a moment of reality to confront. Jack had moved in; this, now, was where he lived. It was done. It was no longer an interesting idea for Mimi to think about, it was another living, breathing human being who was not going to go away after the love-making was over. They went to bed and made the love-making last as long as possible.

On Sunday they got up late and shared the making of breakfast. Eggs, toast, coffee. Mimi did not usually eat breakfast. She didn't know whether Jack usually ate breakfast. It seemed the right thing to do. It was what people did. While she was making breakfast ('How well done do you like your toast?') the unreality settled over Mimi. She performed a play about a couple living together. Breakfast, a shared bath had a dreamlike quality with the Mimi who usually lived in the flat looking on curiously from a distance. After the bath there was another silence. They went back to bed and got up again sometime in the afternoon, when Mimi, trying to shake reality together said, 'I'm going to work for a while.'

This was what she had imagined about being with Jack when they were living apart. How it might work. How it might be extraordinary if it did work. All the time in the world for loving each other, and also, time in the imagination being of a fluid and indeterminate consistency, all the time in the world for silence – her silence which he said he wanted so much, that she would share with him. Peaceful times together, when she would work, planning, cutting and sewing, and he would read and think himself into the project, the one that eluded him, which was what he was really about. Now it was to begin.

Mimi sat at her work table with half a dozen swatches of fabric, fingering them almost absent-mindedly. She was waiting for Jack's presence on her and in her to leave, for the residue of sexual and domestic activity to drain down and let her get back to the usualness of herself with herself. Jack came into the room.

'Hi.'

She waited, thinking he had a question to ask, where something was.

'What are you doing?' he said, standing by the glass doors staring out into the garden.

'Working,' she said.

'Oh.'

A few more minutes silence.

'Are you going to do some work?' she asked him.

'Where?'

'You can set your computer up on the table in the living-room.'

He made a face. It wouldn't do.

'Why don't I use that?' He pointed to a table that had some fabric books on it. 'That would do.'

'But the table in the living-room's big enough.'

'The living room's too . . . public. Why don't I work in here?'

'With me?'

'That would be all right.'

And this was when it dawned on her, two days after he moved in, that whatever he thought he wanted, he could not be alone, or even perhaps, allow her to be.

'You're planning to work in here?' she asked, confirming the obvious.

'There's enough room. You can make your clothes while I sit at the desk, can't you?'

Eventually, after two weeks she told him she couldn't. He took it well enough, though she was left with a sense that she had deprived him of something. The point was, however, that he could even have *thought* it would be all right to share a room, that being on one's own was not a necessity. It was too late to announce that she'd made a mistake, and they continued to enjoy their unlimited passion, but Mimi knew it wasn't going to work, never mind forever, not even for long.

Even so, it had lasted two years, though largely because Jack didn't like disrupting his life until he was ready to do so. After the rampant sex had settled into something a little more regular, Mimi saw increasingly how Jack used and put up with a flawed domestic arrangement while searching for a way out. Gradually, she watched how she became a replacement for Tricia, and could imagine only too easily how Jack received photocopy reps. Probably Jack had first been unfaithful to her a year after the day he had moved in. For him it was a cycle of disappointment. For her, too, even though, not having professed a belief in their undying love, she had nothing really to be surprised about. But then surprise and disappointment could co-exist well enough.

The thing was, Mimi thought, turning over on to her side and hauling the duvet up so that only the top of her head was visible, she hated being lied to. She hated, to be accurate, being someone that someone else lied to. She had made Jack promise right at the beginning that he would never lie to her; that he'd tell her if he was seeing someone else, because she'd rather know than be deceived. Jack had said he would, telling her his first lie. But in any case, they had the project of the two of them going. To sleep with anyone else – for either of them to sleep with anyone else – would have made a nonsense of their being together. He told her about his tomcatting with Tricia because he wanted her to know

126

what he was capable of, and how far he was from that with her. She was different. They were different.

'Even so,' she said. 'Don't lie to me when . . . if you do.'

But, of course, Mimi had lied to him from the day after he had moved in.

'Yes, I love you. Yes, this is good being together. Yes, I'm happy with you.'

None of these reassurances, these love murmurings, were quite true. Sometimes they were fairly true, but always there was an unspoken clause: '. . . but I wish you'd never moved in.' She never said it, not even to herself. Instead, she took to falling into dreamless, storyless sleep.

It was midday already. Mimi heard the letter-box in the hall clink and the afternoon post land. Though she hadn't eaten since she first woke, she didn't feel hungry. Perhaps a cup of tea, she thought, testing herself, and found she would have liked one if she hadn't wanted to stay as she was just at the moment. A little later. There was no hurry. She wouldn't be getting up today. If she found she wanted to get up, well and good, she would; if not, she would potter off to the kitchen and make a cup of tea when she really wanted one and then get back into bed with it. There was no hurry. No hurry at all. For all that midday had crept up on her unawares, the evening seemed to lie on the far side of an inordinate expanse of time.

The bedroom walls were painted a deep green, bluishly tinged, the shade of forests or wet seaweed, either of which provided a perfect ambience for languor. With the duvet pulled up over the jut of her chin, gazing non-specifically ahead of her, she might have been a hermit of the woods, or a reclusive mermaid inhabiting an underwater grotto. The wooden venetian blinds, deep blue, shaded greenishly, looked out on back gardens, so there was very little noise; just occasional shrieks of merriment or cries of dismay of children too young yet to be at school. She let their sounds be the bird calls they resembled if heard with an unprejudiced ear, or if her taste was more marine, then they

127

might be dolphin clicks or whale song with a little extra effort of the imagination.

Mimi had firmly believed in mermaids as a child. In the bath she would make a lozenge shape between her legs and, heels together, toes apart, created, it seemed at the time, a perfect tail, which by resting on her forearms floated very satisfactorily in the water. Remembering, she made the same shape with her legs under the duvet. Like that. She didn't believe in mermaids any more, but she still felt a little mermaidish as she did it. She made the number 4 by bending her left leg so the sole of the foot met the other straightened leg at right angles to its knee. Or would it be a more stylish 4 if she overlapped the foot, resting her ankle on the patella? More 4ish, she decided, trying it, but less comfortable. She returned to the former position, which was restful. Later, she thought, she would reverse the position of her legs, just for symmetry's sake, even if the 4 it made would be no more than a mirror image of the written sign. Never mind. Mirror images were inevitable with asymmetrical figures. Thinking about it, 4 was the only number she could make with her legs, unless she accepted a version of 7 which depended on ignoring the bent leg above the knee, or 9 using the same formation, and not minding the triangularity of the top semi-circle. For a moment she thought about adding 11 to her repertoire, but realized there was no chance of making her legs parallel enough to serve. Which brought her to the possibility of letters; clearly V was perfectly achievable, looked at it from one's own head's point of view. P worked in the same way that 9 did, which was with a bit of imagination. O, also, was not perfect, but might do at a pinch. T was possible if the legs could be counted only from the knees down. And that, as far as she could see, was that. What message could she send with just those figures: OPT, POT, TOP, TO, TV, POV, 794? No very significant statement could be made. *Opt to pot*; good advice for a snooker player, possibly. *TV to pot*; if she fancied exercising her critical faculty. *Top TV*; if she wanted to give herself an argument. *Opt POV*; assuming some media type was hovering in the heavens to read her message. Probably there were phone numbers she might make by repeating 7, 9 and 4 in various combinations. If she was in luck, she might get emergency assistance, or a pizza, or a book delivered, but the chances were very slim. And anyway, having conveyed the number she wanted her overhead reader to call, how would she let him or her know, for example, which emergency service, flavour or title she wanted sent. *Pot*, she might signal, for pot luck, but having taken all that trouble she felt she wanted more than someone else's choice of a good snack or read to be delivered to her bedside. And, of course, what with all those ceilings and floors above her, and the general lack of hovering helpers to signal to, her efforts, however cunningly contrived, would go unnoticed.

Having taken a little exercise, she let her legs splay comfortably, and bringing her arms outside the duvet, folded them restfully over her chest. She took a deep breath and wished she had some scent that smelled of forest or sea to spray around the room, though she doubted any were available that weren't so ersatz they would more likely persuade her she was in the bathroom or the furniture (knotty pine section) department of Selfridges. Perhaps she could make it her life's work to capture the smell of the sea, the real smell of the sea and bottle it for those with sea-green rooms who wished to avoid the trouble and expense of travel, but nonetheless craved ozone. But it took years and years, she understood, to become a parfumier of distinction, and she was making no plans today, so she let the idea drop.

Still, as life-work went, it seemed no sillier than being a dressmaker whose designs mocked the very idea of design, turning out clothes nuns and Greek widows would have found acceptable. Not that nuns or the majority of Greek widows could have afforded her clothes. Her clients paid a high premium for radical simplicity (though not as high as they would have had to pay for an equivalent Japanese simplicity). They found it reassuring. How else could two blunt tipped triangles of rough black stuff have been considered *design*? It was the cut, they told themselves and their friends, such geometrical or shapeless simplicity requires extraordinary cutting skills. The way the clothes hung, seemingly like rags on dummies, could only be achieved with consummate and subtle art. The plainer the clothes, the more awed were Mimi's clients. As a matter of fact, Mimi did have great skill in cutting fabric, but she did not use it in the making of her clothes. A rhomboid was a rhomboid, a lopsided triangle a lopsided triangle. Such cutting required the proficiency learned at nursery school. Rough, untreated material was no more than that. You could play a little with textures – turn the fabric this or that way round and make inside out – but sacking was sacking. Without her high prices, Mimi's customers would have thought themselves cheated. What, only £25 for that shift? Why, I saw one the other day at Yamomoto for £400 – you should have seen the cut!

It wasn't Mimi's aim to deceive her clients – her original intention had been to produce clothes that were beautiful because they were stark and simple, and were simple because they *were* simple. The arcane twist had been added by those wishing for everything – including the simple – to be more complex and harder to achieve. Mimi did not argue with them. She made the frocks and sold them at prices people wanted to pay for them. Sometimes, though, she just wanted to stay in bed. At present there were three outfits hanging in her workroom in various stages of being finished, but her clients, appreciating the workmanship and originality of her designs as they did, were not inclined to hurry her. And she was not inclined to hurry, not today.

I do love lying down, Mimi thought with a slow flush of wonder as idea and its achievement came together in an access of delight. The feeling was so physical, the prolonged suspension of activity – the doing of it, the anticipation of more to come – that there had to be something chemical, some brain change occurring in her. Endomorphs, no, *endorphins*, she corrected herself. End . . . ogenous m . . . orphin . . . e, she undid the neologism and came to an exact description of what she was experiencing. Lightly drugged, on the blurry edge of trance. Medical uses of non-endogenous morphine: post-operative. To inhibit pain. Now how did it do that? By increasing the pleasure to submerge pain, as black paints out white? Was the white still there under the black? No pain. That was what she was feeling. No pain in the nicest possible way. She pictured her brainwaves trickling across graph paper as gently as the sleepy swell of contentment washing through her. Change of mind. No, thank you, Doctor, I've got my own.

However much present pleasure Mimi took in her self-conscious lie-in, some out-of-bed activities were unavoidable. The pressure on her bladder demanded relief. She threw back the duvet and shuffled off to the bathroom, wearing just her T-shirt, not bothering with a dressing gown. There was still a faint odour in the air, the remains of last night's vomiting. A sour high note among the regular bathroom smells that reminded her in its tenacity of that other staying, powerful odour his fingers had carried the night before. The scent of Jack expelling his insides lingered longer, overriding the smell of his aftershave, like the hint of the stink of death we all try to mask with simulated smells of nature at its sweetest. Marketable, maybe, Mimi thought, having caught Jack's entrepreneurial cast of mind, beginning to release the contents of her bladder in a slow, satisfying stream. Some fiendish concoction of sexual and other involuntary bodily emissions to arouse the nose sensitive to the darker excitements. Parfumiers made scents called 'Poison' or 'Egoiste', using a heavy, cloying sweetness to exploit the ambiguity of desire. 'Corruption' might be as well marketed, making explicit the close links between its abstract and material meanings. Call it 'A Hint of Death', 'Decay', 'Distrust', 'Betrayal'. But Mimi shook her head, the times militated against such overt statements of the more shadowy human tendencies. 'Perversion' would have a limited market, no matter what its boycotters did in the secrecy of their lives. Nowadays it was 'Eternity' and 'Escape', as if for all the world human nature had taken a turn for the better. The world should smell her bathroom and her lover's fingers – they should check Mimi's pulse as she smelt them, and wonder what its sudden acceleration had to do with 'Eden'.

Mimi's trickle came to a natural end and she wiped herself dry.

131

She considered the washbasin and whether she should brush her teeth and splash her face. It would make her feel better, she automatically thought, but retorted to herself that she wasn't feeling bad, and if she felt much fresher she might find herself getting up and dressed. She didn't, just at the moment, want to feel that fresh, so she retained the furry laminate of plaque on her teeth and the grit of sleep in a corner of her left eye and returned to bed, plumping up the pillow and giving the duvet a fattening shake. As she got back in, her toes tangled with something at the end of the bed. Her knickers, she recollected, discarded during the gloomy revels of the early hours. 'Tainted Knickers' was another scent which would never make it in the commerical world. She left them where they were. Being with other people had its enjoyable moments, but staying in bed was more reliably pleasurable, Mimi decided, and snuggled down, sleep-driven again, undercover.

Bella

Due to the speed with which news of such a rare turn of events spread through the community, it took remarkably little time before Bella's affliction was recognized as a sign of her sanctity. Before that, it was only Mel who noticed Bella's silence again, when she went upstairs to return the money she'd borrowed. Even then, she didn't think very much of it, having her mind distracted by Davy's continuing and worsening chesty cough and the fact that she'd left him alone while she ran upstairs to pay Bella back. But when she handed Bella the money at her door, Bella said nothing, though she tried for a bit of a smile in the way of a thank you.

'Are you all right?' Mel asked, frowning.

Bella had nodded dismissively, though a 'Yes' would have been more reassuring. Mel saw that she was wearing several layers of woollies and that, again, the fire was not on. Bella herself looked terribly pale and drawn as if she hadn't slept or eaten properly for some time, and the rims of her lower eyelids were an enraged and swollen red.

'Are you sure?' Mel asked, quite alarmed, and taking a step towards Bella.

Bella made a single, deep, assertive nod and another attempt at a smile while Mel hesitated. She wanted to go into Bella's room and have a bit of a chat with her, see what was up – she was a strange bird, but not as strange as this usually – but the thought of Davy alone downstairs stopped her.

'I've left him . . . he's no better. Kept me up all night, coughing. Why don't you come downstairs and have a cup of tea?'

Bella shook her head and pressed Mel's hand between hers to say she wouldn't but that she was all right. 'I'll come up later,' Mel said, but Davy's cough seemed even worse when she'd got downstairs and she had to get him to the afternoon surgery.

The following day she knocked on Bella's door again, this time with Davy on her hip. She'd intended going in for a chat, but when Bella opened the door as silent as before, she hesitated, worrying almost equally that Bella might infect Davy and that Davy might infect Bella with whatever ailed each of them.

The child was limp with the misery and exhaustion of having been coughing almost continually for several days. The antibiotics the doctor had given Mel weren't having any effect. Bella had heard the child hacking throughout the night. His nose dripped and his eyes ran, and his usually quite chubby cheeks were shadowed and slack. He moaned his distress into his mother's neck. Mel hardly looked better than her son, sleep-hungry and pale.

Bella stood back to let Mel and the boy in.

'It's freezing, Leah, why don't you put your fire on?'

Bella indicated that the layers – she picked up each one to show Mel – were enough for her.

'But even if you're warm enough, it's miserable without a fire. What's the matter with you? Why aren't you speaking?'

Bella made a small shrug and matched it with a baffled smile. She didn't know, her shoulders and mouth said, but she felt all right, she just couldn't talk. She shook her head decisively at the mention of a doctor. She knew it wasn't something medicines would cure. She held out her arms to take Davy, and after a moment's hesitation, Mel passed him over, still a little worried about infection but relieved to have her burden lightened for a few minutes. Davy stared balefully at his mother from Bella's lap, but he was feeling too ill even to grizzle at being exiled from her familiar body. Something green and unhealthy dripped from his nose which Bella wiped away with a tissue from her cardigan pocket.

'I'm knackered,' Mel sighed. 'The doctor says it'll pass, but it's like a bloody nightmare. I've heard of tortures done this way: no sleep, nothing but fear and worry. If I had anything to tell anyone, I'd spill the lot, just to get a couple of hours sleep. I'd make something up. Only this is worse than torture because no one's doing it. There's nothing you can do to get yourself out of it.'

Bella looked sympathetic and stroked the boy's head.

'I know I shouldn't complain. I'm lucky to have him and that he was born all right. I'd be lost without him. Sometimes I wonder what kept me going before he was born – it was so aimless before I had him, on my own . . .'

Mel stopped and regretted what she had said.

'I don't mean . . .' Bella indicated that she wasn't hurt. 'I'm only talking about me. Davy's the first thing of my own. Not just the first person, but the first *thing*. And here I am getting pissed off because he's coughing and keeping me awake. It's criminal, isn't it?'

Bella shook her head and Davy stretched out his arms towards his mother and whined for the safety of her body.

'Come on then, brat, let's have you. It's time for some more medicine – you'd think I was feeding him poison the way he struggles.'

Mel hadn't tried to figure out what, exactly, might be the matter with Leah to cause her to lose her voice. There seemed to be no other symptoms, no pain or anything, so Mel just supposed it was some kind of throat infection. Oddly, she'd enjoyed those few minutes complaining to the silent Leah; there was some comfort gained in getting her moans off her chest while her companion merely mimed her understanding. Leah's silence was in some way heartening, and Mel, at least, felt a bit better when she got downstairs. Leah was certainly peculiar, at least half-way to madness, Mel reckoned. Living alone, doing nothing all day, hardly going out, and keeping herself so much to herself. Mel thought she might have come from some hospital – one of those people who'd been turfed out to live in the community. Yet, the last couple of days, Leah's presence upstairs had felt reassuring to Mel, and her visits were not just dutiful. It wasn't that she

135

thought of Leah as a friend – she was far too remote for that – but she was glad Leah was up there, and for some reason which she couldn't fathom, it was to Leah, rather than the other tenants in the house – who were definitely more *normal* people – that Mel wanted to talk.

Two nights later, Mel was woken once again in the early hours from a drifting half-sleep by Davy coughing. It was the third or fourth time that night, but this time it was different; not just the grinding hack but a hawking, strident noise mixed with a terrible reaching for air which the coughing fit prevented his lungs from taking in. She turned the light on and looked at him next to her in the bed. As she watched, Davy's face reddened and deepened to near purple, and beneath the physical battle between the coughing and his hungry lungs, the child tried to cry out his distress, making matters worse by the extra demand for oxygen his cries required.

Mel's heart bolted and panic took over at the sight of Davy losing the fight to breathe. The coughing and gasping seemed to rise higher and higher in his throat as if his very life was being squeezed upwards and out of his small body. In terror, she snatched him up and ran without thinking why out of her flat and up the stairs to Leah's room. Between her thudding heart and her raging head, she only knew she had to hold him and get help. There was a phone on the landing, but she was too blinded by terror and the need to hold her suffocating child close and safe to operate it. Perhaps, that was why she raced up to Leah and banged on the door with her fist, shouting out her name over and over.

When Bella opened the door, she was fully dressed and had clearly been up and awake even though it was three-thirty in the morning.

'An ambulance . . . please, get an ambulance,' Mel gasped.

Davy was no longer coughing. His mouth was wide open, like a fish drowning on dry land. His whole body had gone into a spasm, unnaturally rigid against Mel's chest. He could no longer fight for air. His eyes bulged wide, and the colour of his face was now more blue than purple.

'He's dying!' Mel screamed. 'Help me!'

Without any clear intention, Mel pushed the stiffened child towards Bella. It was obvious to both women that it was too late to call an ambulance. Davy would die before it could arrive. Mel's cry for help was pure desperation, and pressing Davy into Bella's arms, an instinctive action, wanting someone, anyone, to do something, anything, to save the precious child she could do nothing to help.

Bella took him, her eyes as filled with anxiety as Mel's, but her acceptance of the boy was just as instinctive as his mother's offering of him. Mel stood frozen at the door, and for a moment Bella held the child in her arms, helplessly, not knowing what to do. Then she turned and went to her wooden chair by the table. She sat with her arms enclosing Davy, whose eyes had lost any connection with the world in which the two women existed, and rocked gently with him, backwards and forwards, holding his head against her breast. There was no intention, merely an act of rhythmic stillness in the face of the monstrous, overwhelming storm that was raging. The two women were submerged in the unstoppable moment of the death of a child. They lived in this moment, participants and witnesses of the dying of a life, and yet this moment, the present, was precious because after it would come the future and the inescapable fact of a dead child. Bella might have been trying to rock time to a standstill and Mel stood on the threshold of the room willing her on. For both of them an eternity passed, as if they might have locked forever into the present moment, a hopeless moment with despair on the far side of it, but better to live forever in that one moment, which at least prevented something too terrible to think about from *having happened*. There was no going back, no abolishing the terrible now, so the only hope left was not to go forward.

It took a time which, then or afterwards, neither woman could measure, before they realized that Davy's mouth was closed and his eyes shut, and that he lay, freed from the terrible muscle

137

tension of his spasm, limp now and silent against Bella's heart. They had failed to hold back the future.

Mel took several leaden steps into the room and sank to her knees beside Bella, reaching out to touch her son. Bella, still holding the boy, sat on in defeat, immobilized by exhaustion. Mel stroked Davy's cheek, tears streaming down her face. What she felt caused her to press her palm flat against his skin, then to lay her other hand against his other cheek.

'Leah,' Mel gasped, now bringing her face right up to Davy's. 'Leah, he's not . . . He's asleep. He's just asleep.'

It was true. As Bella looked down at the child, he moved, snuggling himself more comfortably into her lap. Davy was asleep and breathing easily. His cheeks were plump and pink, his runny nose clear, his tight little body completely relaxed. He might have been having a regular afternoon nap except for the stillness of the world around them all at this early hour.

'He's fine, Leah,' Mel breathed, stroking his head and cheeks and shaking her head in wonder. 'He's perfectly all right.'

Davy opened his eyes slowly, roused by his mother's fingers feathering his face. He looked around him at the strange room and then up at the unfamiliar person whose lap he was in. He was not alarmed, just a little confused as any child would be waking in the middle of the night in the wrong place. He stretched out his arms to Mel for her to take him.

'Mummum,' he said, sleepily, dropping his head against his mother's shoulder.

'Leah, what did you do?' Mel whispered.

Bella shook her head and stared blankly at Mel and her little boy. She hadn't done anything.

The next morning Davy was his old young self; a regular, energetic toddler striving for everything he wasn't quite ready to do. There was no sign of his cough and none of the wheezing, mucous chestiness of days past. His illness, and certainly the previous night's emergency, might have been a dream. Mel sat in front of her gas fire, drinking her coffee, watching her healthy son, who for the best part of a week had been clinging on to her, clattering around the room; and she tried to make sense of what had happened.

That Davy had been ill, there was no doubt – her exhaustion was proof of that even if memory wasn't – and that the previous night he had as good as died, choking and suffocating in her arms, was impossible to deny. Not even the worst of her dreams had ever had such searing reality. If the horror of last night was dreamlike in its unfolding, the essential quality of the dream was its dreadful waking actuality. In any case, she had only to go upstairs and check with Leah to confirm what she thought she knew better than anything that had ever happened to her before. Yet Davy now showed no signs of illness, not even the tiredness of recuperation. However real last night had seemed, this morning's ordinary health was realer.

She found herself oddly reluctant to go upstairs and see Leah. Perhaps it was that she wanted to hold on to this morning's normality rather than revive last night's emergency. Would seeing Leah break the spell? Was *this* the dream – the most wished-for dream possible: that Davy was fine? If she went upstairs, it seemed to Mel that she risked reality turning on her and becoming the nightmare after all. It was better, if this was a dream, to let it continue for as long as it could; the alternative was the future they had so desperately wished against the night before. Davy's sudden recovery had the unreality of a dream, but please let it go on, Mel prayed, even if it wasn't true.

'Davy,' she called softly to the boy who was rolling around on the floor being an imaginary beast from the dawn of time. She held out her arms for him to come to her, and he scrambled up and locked his mother in a brief embrace before wriggling away and setting off back to prehistory. He had felt and smelled real enough for the moment he was in her arms: soft and warm, a living creature exuding a sweet scent that was utterly different from the acrid, sickly odour of the days before.

Mel would have put it all down to the miracle of antibiotics, except that several days had passed since they had been expected to work, and not even antibiotics could account for the chasm between the horror of the child's condition a few hours ago and his present health and energy. No one in Mel's experience had ever got better that fast. But what else apart from medication was there to put it down to? Mel was not a believer in magic – she'd spent too much time and far too much energy struggling to achieve her basic needs to believe in supernatural intervention. Sometimes people helped each other out as best they could, and very occasionally, if you worked hard at it, social services came up with a little extra, but outside those not very reliable circles of safety, you were on your own. No one, no thing, was watching out to keep life fair and decent, or to keep little boys from dying. So Mel spent most of the day in her room, just being with Davy, calling to him and holding on to him for as long as he'd let her, and cherishing the fact of his being there, with her, alive and well. It wasn't until the late afternoon that she finally made herself go upstairs to Leah's room.

She stood outside the door with Davy wriggling on her hip aching to get free to slither over the linoleum floor, but she hesitated before knocking, feeling suddenly ashamed to have waited so long to thank Leah. Or so she put it to herself. Her reluctance was to finding herself once again in Leah's room, the three of them; a repetition that might negate the hours of this extraordinary day and put everything back to what last night had seemed inevitable.

There was no answer to her knock, but Mel knew Leah was in. Though she hadn't consciously been listening, she realized that she hadn't heard Leah's footsteps on the stairs. Perhaps she was asleep. Carefully, holding tightly on to Davy with one arm, she tried the door handle.

Bella was standing by the window, seeming to look out, though darkness had fallen over the winter afternoon and from her window there was nothing to see except the outline of the disused bottling factory across the road. The room was in darkness, so that Bella was just a shadow among shadows in the room, as still as her dark wardrobe or the table with the bible lying open on it in,

Mel realized, the same position as it had been last night. For a moment, Mel thought of silently shutting the door and creeping back downstairs, but then was once again ashamed.

'Leah,' she called softly.

Bella turned at the sound of the voice, before her eyes and mind had had time to change to suit the new circumstance of no longer being alone. Her eyes were still focused for the middle-distance, for looking through the pane of glass and seeing nothing, and her face was in a mournful repose, numbed and absent.

'Look, he's fine,' Mel said, entering the room with her squirming son.

Bella's face also entered the room, and she smiled at the child as Mel let him down to crawl on the floor. Bella turned on a table lamp and the two women stood watching Davy's investigations for a moment.

'Last night,' Mel said. 'What happened?'

Bella looked at Mel and then sat herself in the chair in which, last night, she had cradled Davy. She gave Mel a wide eyed, open-handed shrug of helplessness. It confirmed for Mel that she had not dreamed the night before, but didn't go any way to answering the deeper question.

'What's wrong with your voice?'

Bella couldn't say.

Suddenly, Mel felt something sharp surge inside her, akin to anger, though perhaps it was nearer to panic. It sounded in the timbre of her voice.

'What did you *do* last night?'

It was ridiculous that Mel should feel rage at Bella for having saved her son's life, and that was not what her sudden fierceness was about, of course. It came from an inability to conceal from herself that her son's life had been almost lost and then saved, and both in a manner which made no sense. The question of *what* had happened was no longer the subterfuge her mind used to cover the real question of *how* it happened. If Davy's death had been halted by medicine or surgery, Mel would have been thankful and weak with relief, but Davy's death had been halted, just that, with no

141

intervening logic to make it understandable. Beneath her gratitude for Davy's life, Mel was outraged by the incomprehensible, seemingly accidental nature of his sudden recovery. In some way, the sickening pointlessness of the near tragedy was intensified by the absence of a rational explanation for its having been averted. If Bella had been incomprehensibly responsible for saving Davy's life, then she must also take on the burden of it having been incomprehensibly at risk.

'What did you *do* last night?'

The question extended itself back in time to take in the scandal of innocent suffering.

As if from outside the force of her anger, Mel heard the terrible accusation in her voice, and was shocked by it. How could she be feeling like this towards the woman who had helped her? How could she speak to her in such a tone?

Bella, however, understood it very well, and felt no animosity towards Mel for voicing the bafflement and dismay she herself had been oppressed by since last night's events. Davy had been dying in her arms, perhaps had even been dead, and then he was healthy and alive, though that did not describe accurately the lack of sequence of events. There had been no *first* and *then*. The event of Davy being peacefully asleep and well had not come after his awful struggle against death. It was separate, not consequential. It might even have been simultaneous. It seemed so to Bella. The sleeping child had *replaced* the dying child, as if time had reiterated itself and told a different story altogether. Only in the logical light of day did there appear to have been a chronology, but Bella knew better, and so did Mel, which accounted for her distress.

What had Bella done? It was the question she had been staring after as she looked through her blank window for all those hours since the event, seeing nothing, because there was nothing to see. Bella had not done anything, only held the boy, stunned at her helplessness and the catastrophe of a young, unused life slipping away. Nothing, nothing, she wanted to say with the voice which would not come. Something happened, but I did nothing. Yet, although this was true, she also knew that Davy had come alive in her arms and against her ticking heart, and without beginning to see how, she was certain that it had happened in some way through her. And this was the cause of her dismay. What she could not deny in her mind, she would have denied with her voice: yet that voice, that opportunity to refute the monstrosity of having had a hand in reclaiming a life, had been denied her. Her voice had been stopped, she had not been permitted to escape from what had happened. Who had denied her, what had refused permission? Something that was punishing her for her empty, unbelieving faith; something that acted against her for dragging it into existence, for bringing it to life with her cold and calculating choice. Something whispered in her ear: *you think, therefore I am, and there'll be no denying it.*

Mel suppressed her anger, as she had to since it made no sense and had no use. Simple gratitude and less simple wonder replaced the unmanageable outrage. She did not use the word 'miracle' to anyone, but when she spoke of Davy's recovery to her friends the word hung in the air. Mel continued not to believe in religious dogma, but that she had witnessed some kind of intervention, though she had no name for it, she could not doubt. It gave her description of what had happened a fuzzy enough boundary for listeners to draw their own conclusions. Mel needed to describe what had happened, though she spoke only to a couple of people and her doctor, as a child needs a problematical event in its life to be told and re-told in order to absorb it. It was not possible for Mel simply to let it go, nor to keep Bella out of the story. It was in her arms that her son had come alive again.

The doctor, of course, put it down to the antibiotics, though he admitted it was odd they should have kicked in so much later than expected. Perhaps the child was not as ill as Mel had supposed. Though he did not say so, he knew only too well how stressed and anxious parents overestimated the degree of their children's illness. It was true, however, that Mel's description of Davy losing the fight for breath was a clinically accurate picture of a life-threatening emergency.

The surgery nurse and receptionist passed the story on, though Davy's GP would have preferred to let the matter drop. Mel's best friend told her sister, who mentioned it at the playgroup she worked in. The story came to the ears of Mr Amin, the sub-postmaster, who incorporated the wonder of it into his amiable chat with his customers. Within a week or two, the area was buzzing with the news of the strange woman many suddenly remembered having seen around, who had stopped talking or been struck dumb, and then performed a miracle by bringing a small child back from the dead.

In what was generally acknowledged to be the most secular society in Western history, word spread like an airborne disease. If the churches were far from full and the majority had no interest whatsoever in the complexity of modern theology with its denials and rationalizations, this did not mean that the original impulse towards religious belief had vanished without trace. Whatever their difficulties and degrees of cynicism, people liked the idea of a God who made things better, who made things fairer. It was, after all, the fact that things had so stubbornly not got better or fairer which had caused so many to shrug off their faith. It was true that the mosques were fuller, but their faithful too were pleased to see a sign in a world where signs were sorely lacking. The mixed community felt it was about time that God stood up amongst them, on their side, to be counted, and no one was much concerned about the doctrinal or medical niceties.

Bella noticed the strangeness around her when she went to cash her giro-cheque at the post office a day or two after Davy's recovery. Heads turned and voices lowered to a busy hum as she passed, people on the other side of the street actually stopped walking and stared at her, pointing her out to their friends. She feared there was something wrong, that she had forgotten, perhaps, to put on a vital item of clothing, or worse, that she was talking to herself in the way crazy people do without being aware of it.

When she opened the door of the newsagents', at the back of which was the post-office counter, there was an immediate hush.

All transactions and conversation came to a halt and people turned to look at her as she made her way nervously to the back of the shop to Mr Amin's counter. She slid her book through the gap in the protective glass. Mr Amin clasped his hand together, and then, before she could retract it, he pressed both his palms over her hand, imprisoning it and her giro in post-office territory.

'It was a wonderful thing you did,' he told her, his eyes gleaming with admiration. 'It was more than wonderful. It was a miracle.'

The word had been spoken. It came at Bella like the blow she had been trying to avoid; a wallop of a word she had been refusing admittance for days now. She had remained indoors and shut down her mind to keep out the memory of Davy and that night. Several times there had been knocks on the door, and Mel's voice calling out her name – 'Leah' – the wrong name to emphasize the wrongness of what had happened. Of course, Bella was pleased the little boy had recovered, yet there was, to her, something dangerous and malevolent about the manner in which it had happened. She understood perfectly that the child coming alive in her lap – there was no doubt in her mind that he had been dead – was a form of punishment. A most terrible retribution. Like any kind of shame, Bella tried to conceal it from herself, to keep the event from swirling around in her mind and making her reel with the disgrace of it. That was what it was: the very opposite of grace. Disgrace had come down on her in the guise of a miracle. That it seemed to others to partake of divine intervention and that she was the conduit, was the very essence of the punishment.

Intervention it was, certainly. Bella herself had done nothing. She had sat with the lifeless child in her lap in lowest depths of despair. There had been no hope, no wish, no possibility of prayer. She made no attempt to intercede on behalf of the crime against humanity that had occurred in her arms, for she knew there was nothing and no one to direct her plea towards. In all the empty universe there was nothing but the misfortune of one tiny tragedy, among many more, multiplied by millions upon millions, that went unnoticed by the implacable nothingness in

145

which she had chosen to place her bitter belief. And then beyond the scandal of the death of a small, young life, the even greater scandal of a resurrection had been committed. She had created her deity and it had taken its most dire revenge by making her its chosen one.

Of course, Bella was not the only one who would suffer from this brush with the miraculous. Davy would remember nothing of the events of that night, but Mel had it in her mind with every breath she saw him take. Soon after the miracle had occurred, Mel had moved to another city, away from the talk and the rumours. Away, also, from the perpetrator. She kept herself to herself, fearing that if she got too close to anyone she might find herself telling the story of her son's miraculous escape from death. She would never speak of it to Davy – in all his life he never heard Leah's name – but nevertheless to Mel he would always be a child who had been saved from the jaws of death, a life so special and precious because she had nearly lost it that she would never be able to relinquish a certain wonder and gratitude that resonated in her voice as she spoke to him, gleamed from her eyes when she looked at him and vibrated through her nerves as she touched and held him.

There would always be the question of why. Davy had been saved, and not by any ordinary, understandable human effort. All through Davy's childhood Mel would be searching for the reason, waiting to understand what it was her son had been saved *for*. Although her attitude to life had not changed for herself, she could not help heaping an undefined expectation on her son which was to burden him all his days. The expectation would seep into him, so that he, too, came to sense he was waiting to find out something. Whatever he did, he would feel it was not enough, could never be enough, though why he felt this way, he would never know. It would curse the ordinariness of his life – to leave school, find a job, marry, have children, would never sit right with him. He would grow from an agitated child into a restless young man unable to settle to anything and whose search for what he never understood and could never name would slide into an aimless wandering, a nervy dissatisfaction with himself and his lot. He was convinced something had to *happen* to him, that anything he actually did himself might interfere with his destiny. So he did nothing, and waited for his life to begin.

He would leave Mel while he was still very young and take to squats and then the streets. His mother was too much of a burden, her anticipatory eyes, her curious and respectful distance. Davy had to leave her, though he would never manage to get away from the undefined demand of her almost reverential gaze. Mel would be left to grow old in her self-imposed isolation, baffled, alone with the knowledge of what had happened to Davy and the unaccountable consequence – for how could such a thing be without consequence? – of her resurrected son's shiftless and pointless existence.

But for the present the consequences were all for Bella. There was no escaping the word 'miracle' once it floated free in the air. Bella's silence confirmed the non-accidental nature of what had happened.

'She's been struck dumb,' people in the locality said to each other meaningfully, as if such signs were a regular and understood part of the spiritual fabric of late twentieth-century life. 'She brought a kiddie back to life.' The deed and its significance were accepted with remarkably little question. The two-thousand-year and more distance between a time of miracles and the present time of cause and effect; the space between the superstitious belief of the ancients and the supercilious rationality of the moderns; both sets of distinctions collapsed as if nothing more held them apart than the lack of a local event. The desire to take up the miracle that had happened amongst them was overwhelming – not, of course, to the local doctors, or the few academics who were beginning to move into the area, but to the young and the old, both burdened by disappointment and a dim future, to the middle-aged who found themselves frightened and insecure; to the generality of people who found nothing more exciting in their lives than television and popular scandal offered by the papers, this was something extraordinary that had happened in real life in

147

a street they knew, to people they saw as they went about their daily routine, people they could reach out and touch. It was theirs. In their time and their place. One child had not died. There was somebody among them. Something special had come to them, to their own streets, and done something about the inevitable. Belief was there, ready and waiting; all it needed was a sign. A child had not died. A woman who was all but invisible to the remote world of fame and fortune had been struck dumb and performed a miracle in Bradley Street. That was, at last, something to believe in.

Very soon people were no longer just staring and talking about Bella from a distance. On the street, people came and, like Mr Amin, clasped her hand. She would flinch from the uninvited contact, and stare helplessly at them as they palpated her flesh. It was enough to touch, and her silence was only confirmation of what they had heard; verifying her power. The alarm in her eyes did not register with the people who grasped at her, or if they saw the tragic look in her eyes they mistook it for sympathy and understanding. Gradually, Bella's top-floor room in Bradley Street became a place of pilgrimage. People in trouble trod the steps up to her door with sick children, intractable diseases, desperate sorrows. She opened her door to their knocks to see strangers imploring her to do something – whatever it was she did – for them. Bella's silence disappeared under the sound of pleas for help, for more miracles. She still had no voice and could only shake her head at them with an increasingly haunted look in her eyes. She could not explain that she had done nothing, that, if anything, something had been done to her. She was more powerless than the most deprived and distressed supplicant who came to her for help. She could not tell them that she was not refusing, as her shaking head suggested, but simply incapable of doing what they believed she could do. Eventually, Bella stopped answering her door and kept it bolted. She hid in her room like an outlaw. People looked stunned as they turned away, taking their problems back home with them. They needed her only to make a gesture, to extend a hand, to hold a child, to nod at them; these things would have made them feel they too shared in her specialness, might even, in some cases, have alleviated their troubles. They were confused. They had come to her. What more did they have to do but believe in her? They began to feel they had been cheated. Some terrible trick had been played on them. Mel and Davy had left. The evidence of the miracle had vanished. Perhaps the whole thing was a hoax. A cruel joke by a wicked woman who was laughing at them.

The local people looked at her with sullen glares now when, eventually, Bella ventured out in need of food. And then voices were raised, resentful and abusive. Belief turned sour and transformed into hatred. Mr Amin handed her her money in an accusing silence, while at the back of the post-office queue someone hissed that she had no right to money from the State, *their* money, after what she'd done, the way she'd made fools of poor and needy people. Bella felt all this to be as inevitable as rain falling. This had to be the outcome, from the moment Davy had opened his eyes in her arms.

Late one night, Bella dressed in as many warm layers as she could, stuffed the rest of her clothes into a plastic carrier bag, and walked away from Bradley Street. She took only what was essential. Behind her, on the table in her vacated room, she left the keys and her bible.

For years now Bella had been wandering. For how many years? Who could remember? Years lacking markers pass stealthily; without Christmas, birthdays, holidays (what, another year gone by already?), time becomes erratic, positively eccentric. She would overhear someone mention the date: 1993, and doubt her hearing before she doubted her mind. It was 86, or 87 at the latest. Surely? But once she found no reason not to accept what she had heard, she let the intervening absent years drop away with a shrug. 'It's 1993,' she'd tell herself, repeating the information several times to get it firmly into her head. Next thing, someone was saying it was 1995. Something else to memorize.

The seasons weren't much use for keeping track of time.

Spring, summer, autumn and winter seemed to have lost their places. Mostly, it was cold, sometimes it was very cold, every now and again it was much too hot. Bella had no recollection of it ever being just right. There wasn't any obvious order to cling on to. Nor any point in trying to cling on to it. What difference did it make to her what the date was?

There was a kind of regularity of place about her life. It was inevitable since her range was limited by the availability of soup kitchens and the handful of hostels. There were places she arrived at again and again over the years; faces which greeted her, as they handed her a hunk of bread, in such a way that suggested they might have recognized her – from yesterday or last year – even if she didn't know them from the devil. An entrance to a disused cinema was open at certain times and a vat of soup was ladled into polystyrene cups for those who turned up. Sometimes she found herself there in time to get soup, sometimes arrived to find nothing but big black doors locked shut and a dilapidated sign saying BINGO written across them. She could never figure out what the routine was, and soon she didn't try. She would just shuffle there and shuffle away again if nothing was on offer. Her legs were programmed by now. She didn't have to have a destination, the legs took care of it. They just walked around and around as if they were the wheels of a train sliding along rails (some wheels, some slide). The soup kitchens and hostels just appeared, and the legs knew to stop and check if there was anything doing before shunting off again on their pointless journey. Bella's mind recognized only the smell of food, or the milling about of down-and-outs that signified a place to sleep. She might have been there yesterday, even every day for years, however many years it was, but she was only interested in what these places did, not whether she had been there before. What did it matter? For all she knew or cared her wanderings could have taken in the entire known universe, or merely a half a square mile or so of familiar London streets. What did it matter? She had other things to think about, if thinking was what she wanted to do. Which was not necessarily the case.

Of course, she cherished her non-recognition of people and places. Familiarity was fraught with dangers. She did not want to know or be known by people and she achieved an anonymity that allowed her to take soup from offering hands without any other contact being made, or sit sometimes around a vagrants' fire without ever speaking or being spoken to. She no longer knew whether she still lacked the power of speech, she never tried it out. If someone in authority approached her she just looked down at the pavement and shook her head from side to side and eventually they left her alone. Her fellows around their fire simply accepted that she didn't speak, though sometimes one might talk in her vicinity, as if she were an audience for their woes. She never responded in any way to their monologues, she never even heard them, taking them as noise, like the wind or the sound of rain guttering from an overflowing pipe. When they had finished the noise stopped and nothing had altered. Intermittently, after sitting at a fire that had become embers, a body would press against hers and push her to the ground. Not roughly, it was more like the toppling of a pile of rags, an unsteadying that left her on her back with the weight of another on top of her. There'd be fumbling and mumbling, as her assailant struggled with her layers of clothing, not attempting to take them off, but only to find a way through beneath them. Then he'd grumble some more at the trouble it took to find a way through to his own body. Bella would lie still and wait for it all to be done, which it was very quickly once he had heaved his bulk on top of her and finally positioned his half-hearted member at the entrance to her barely recollected vagina. It was over in a grunt and a squirm, sometimes before he'd found his way inside. This also altered nothing. Bella had no idea whether it occurred around the same fire, or different ones. She might have had a regular lover, or an unrepeating series of them. When it was over, Bella would wait for him to roll off her, and then get herself upright and standing in stages. Once she was up, she moved off without so much as a glance at her lover who lay snoring where he had dropped. No words ever passed between them, nor even any physical contact except for the barest

151

minimum collision of their most anonymous parts.

She was free of everything that might go wrong or prove difficult in a life, and once she had built up the layers of fabric around her as protection against the weather, and her body adjusted to the cycles of discomfort, she found the life to be acceptable. She was frequently hungry, often cold, sometimes ill; but all the sensations and pangs occurred at a distance that was peculiarly untroubling. She learned not to take them personally, not to mind, just as she no longer minded being drenched in a downpour. Underneath her layers of protection her body performed what it had to, and that, too, was of no interest to her. Discomfort and shame became shadows and finally disappeared. There must have been a time, early on in her street life, when she tried to maintain her decency, but it proved too difficult and then, once she had failed often enough, unnecessary. The unthinkable became thinkable through force of circumstances. The transition had been so easy that no memory of it remained.

She never thought of the past. There had been a woman with a home and a husband and the fear of losing them. There had been a woman with a child, and the terror of having to look after someone else. There had been a woman who had walked away, become changed and found a strategy for existing that had turned on her. She never thought about them. They never troubled her to be remembered. But then, one day, long after she had forgotten what she no longer wanted to remember, there was a boy. He stopped and squatted in front of a fire at which Bella had settled herself. The others became uneasy, and drifted off. He was too young, not like them, the sort that preyed on ageing drunks and derelicts, taking their last possessions and taunting them or worse, just for the fun of it, just to show their superiority. Bella didn't move. She neither noticed the boy's arrival nor the others' departure.

'Not scared of me, then?' the boy asked her.

Another voice. She paid it no heed.

'You. Not scared what I might do?'

When she continued to ignore him, he went on like others

did, making his noise in her hearing.

'I could kill you. I could knock you over and kick you to death.
I could turn your face into pulp. I could make your insides mush.
It wouldn't matter. Nobody would care. It wouldn't be any
different if I killed you than if I didn't kill you. No one would
notice. Apart from the mess. But they'd clean that up and throw
the remains of you away and nothing would change. Not one
thing would be different in the world if you were dead. Are you
listening to me?'

The boy took out a leather pouch from the pocket of his jeans
jacket and laid out the makings of a fix on a nearby crate he pulled
over to serve as a table. He worked in silence, concentrating on
the task of preparing the syringe and tightening his belt around
his arm with his teeth to bring up a vein. Soon he sighed, though
too softly to break through Bella's inattention.

'Don't worry,' he addressed Bella's impassive profile again. 'I
won't kill you. There wouldn't be any point. If you had anything,
I'd take it, and I might kill you if you tried to stop me, but look at
you, what have you got that I could want? Killing you wouldn't be
worth the effort. I'll probably kill someone, someday. I'm not
squeamish. It could happen easily. But when I do, it'll be
someone special, not some filthy old fleabag who I wouldn't touch
in case I got a disgusting disease. I wouldn't even let my knife
touch you. I've got one, see?' He pulled a blade from a leather
holster at his waist. 'I keep it for if that's what's going to happen.
Something's going to happen. You, Fleabag, you listening?
Something's going to happen to me. It might be killing someone,
I don't know yet. It could be, or it could be something else. I'm
not just another street junkie. Don't think that. I've got this . . .
destiny. I was born *for* something. It could be anything, I don't
know yet. It'll happen. Whatever it is, it'll happen, and it'll be
big. I've always known that, for as long as I can remember, I've
known it. This feeling. It's my knowledge. That's why I don't
bother with all the ordinary stuff. That wasn't what I was meant
for. All my life, they've looked at me knowing I'm different,
special. There's no point in doing anything but wait. For it to

happen. That's why I'm not going to kill you. I have to wait. I mustn't interfere with my destiny.'

At some point during his rambling speech, the boy's words took on meaning for Bella. She turned to look at him, a fair-haired, emaciated youth, still in his teens, almost a child still, filthy and sullen faced, his blue eyes flickering dimly with the light of the drug he had injected into himself. He felt her looking at him.

'Yeah. Right. You pay attention to me, you filthy old cow. You remember me. This isn't just anyone you're sitting next to. When you hear about me, you remember I talked to you. You think, it was him, the one who sat and talked to me by the fire. Maybe it won't be killing someone, it might be something else. It might be . . . You don't know, it could be anything.'

Bella continued to stare at him as he put away his leather pouch and stood up, looming over her, holding his knife in front of her face.

She croaked out a bare whisper with her unused voice. 'What's your name?'

'Davy. And don't you forget it,' he told her, circling the knife slowly.

Bella continued to sit alone in front of the dying fire long after the boy had left. She had no recollection of having broken her silence. Gradually, a pain began deep inside her in the region of her chest. She was used to discomfort and pain, but this one developed and grew like a drum roll, increasing in intensity with every breath she took. She got up and tried to walk it away. As the night passed she dragged herself along the streets, keeping on the move, but the pain stabbed at her, refusing to be left behind, like a bad memory that wouldn't go away.

She staggered around the whole of the next day, not letting herself stop and rest, fearing if she did so, the pain would never allow her to get up again. It was not a fear of dying that kept her on the move, not even stopping where food and perhaps medical aid were on offer, but a terror of something that seemed to lurk behind the pain itself, as if it were just the outer casing of something more terrible that would break out if her body was at rest. However bad the pain got, and it became very bad, it was necessary to remain upright and keep moving. Her legs shuffled around their familiar circle, without a destination, but with a purpose. Eventually, however, the following evening, they gave out, and Bella's body revolted against the pain. At the back of a cinema behind Camden Town High Street, she came to a halt. The pain was too much, even breathing was too much. Whatever the dangers of stillness and of lying down, she had come to the end of movement. Like a clockwork toy whose mechanism had wound down, she sank to the ground. As soon as she was horizontal, the pain dissipated, drifting away like a cloud called on to rain somewhere else. It had finished with her.

5

'She's alive then?'

Cath looked down at the patient as she spoke to the ward sister.

'You know her?' Sister Fredericks asked.

'I prepped her when she came in last night. Peeled her is more accurate.'

'That couldn't have been pleasant. We still don't know who she is.'

'She isn't anyone,' said Cath taking the medical notes from the foot of the bed. 'The paramedics christened her Bella.'

Sister Fredericks smiled and took the notes from Cath.

'Why not? We've got to call her something.'

She wrote Bella in the space after *Name*, enclosing it in inverted commas.

'She came round a little this morning. But she's not talking to anyone. Poor thing, perhaps she's got nothing to say. The police are trying to identify her for us, but from the state of her, I don't suppose she lives anywhere or knows anyone who isn't in much the same state as herself.'

'What if she gets better?'

The sister shrugged, though not brutally.

'Back out on the streets again, I suppose. They'll try and sort a hostel out for her, but they're usually on the streets again pretty quickly. I expect she'll be back here soon enough, or in the mortuary. Makes you wonder what they're being saved for.' She gave the young nurse a weary look. 'Right. We don't save anyone for anything, we just save them. Or we don't.'

Cath moved to the head of the bed and took a closer look. She was surprised to see her tramp, cleaned up and asleep in crisp hospital sheets, looking like just another very ill patient. Anonymous, but in a different way from the anonymous derelict who had arrived at A & E the night before. She was old, perhaps in her seventies. Her face was grey, though no longer with dirt. The flesh was dull and unreflective, the skin around the jaw and neck coarse and loose. Her hair which had been brushed out, though not washed, was equally dull and coarse, reaching to her shoulders in a straggling mass. A smell of disinfectant came from her reminding Cath of the stench that had wafted up at her the previous night. She looked to Cath as if she was dying. Though she breathed, it came hard and rasping, and there was something moribund about her features that suggested something other than the repose of sleep. Cath noticed how much less of her there was than she had at first supposed. Her body was quite slight under the blankets – the great bundle that had lain on the A & E trolley had been little more than a mass of protective clothing, wound round and round a malnourished frame.

Without warning, the woman's eyes fluttered open and rested incuriously on Cath, accidentally in her line of vision.

'Oh. You're awake. I'm Cath. I was here when they brought you in last night. I came to see how you are.'

The eyes focused slightly and the mouth did something that looked to Cath like an attempt to twist itself into a sneer. She told herself that the woman in the bed was hardly conscious, and was probably unable to make sense of what she heard, never mind sneer at her.

'You're going to be all right, Bella,' Cath said.

The woman closed her eyes and they remained shut.

So Bella's going to be all right, Bella thought. Easy enough for her to say. 'I'm Cath.' That came easy. And I'm Bella, whatever that means. And I'm going to be all right. Whatever that means.

The blankness which Bella woke up to was no more filled in for her having recognized her name. Bella was her, all right, but Bella was a creature of the present, whose existence went no further back than the previous night. She was a name and an anatomy, and, oddly perhaps for someone with no past, it was not enough to be going on with. Behind the identity was an absence, and even in her feeble state, it irritated.

Bella sighed, not knowing what else to do, when suddenly she heard the strains of an old hymn. She recognized it as the tune called Crimond. Well, derelict or not, she'd evidently been a church-goer in her time, though whether for prayer or soup-kitchen she couldn't say. Or perhaps she had only impatiently watched *Songs of Praise* on TV while waiting for something more secular to come on. Whatever, she enjoyed a little break from her fretting, and sang along to the pluck of her heart-strings, now not merely tuning up but playing in harmony.

> *My soul he-ee doth re-e-store ag-ain*
> *And me-ee to walk doth make*
> *Withi-in the paths of ri-i-ghteousness*
> *E'en fo-or his own na-a-mesake.*

'Well, maybe God knows me,' she told herself, as if she might have told herself the same thing many times before, and perhaps, before, might even have believed it.

Maybe she just ought to come to terms (there was a good phrase, where had that come from?) with her lack of past. After all, there was no guarantee that she would live; she'd heard the sister say that. And what was the point of finding herself, the story of herself, if she then died? Not much use to her then, having a past, being a person and not just a name and a body. That was true for everyone, of course, she tried to comfort herself. They could wallow in their past, feel smug about their stories, but in the end they'd all be dead, whoever they were, whatever they'd done. And, pouff, up in smoke the whole shenanigans. Still, it was true that it looked as if she might die sooner than most, so the comfort was more theoretical than consoling.

The possibility that, thanks to the wonders of modern medi-cine, she might not die gave her pause for thought. If she lived, a

159

blank Bella, what would that be like? No one to know, nowhere to go. But it seemed that her past (she must have had one, everyone did) had put her in exactly that position anyway. Pasts don't necessarily *give* you anything. There was the chance that finding out who she was would change nothing. But at least, Bella told herself, it would give her something to tell herself during the empty, shiftless remains of her life. It was the least that everybody else had, apart from a body, and Bella, though she had a body (even if it wasn't much to write home about, where ever that was), wanted the other thing too.

She heard the sound of her visitors walking away and out of her ward with some relief. People standing around one's semi-conscious body, insisting on telling you their names and their part in your life, wondering idly where you'd come from and where you'd be going if you were going any further than the mortuary, was really very taxing for a poor old lady with nothing but a name to hang on to. Unconsciousness, at the moment, seemed a better bet.

Mask

She knew he wouldn't be back. Perhaps because he couldn't be back, or perhaps because he had brought her a present that spoke too loudly. Perhaps it was simply because she had broken the silence. Faceless Bella in her faceless house was no longer waiting. You didn't wait for what you knew was not going to happen. Her condition now was different. Waiting had provided her with a future – he would be coming home, later – even if it didn't include having a plan. They had no plans, her and him, but they had made a future. He had made her a future. Now, he and it were gone.

Time had taken a tumble in that house. Day and night were still important because the atavistic power of light and dark cannot be ignored. In much the same way, they were aware of the change of season. The early morning brightness which spread like butter on the stone wall opposite her bedroom had the very smell of spring about it. The fact that winter had passed was inescapable. But that was all. The daily signals of time – newspapers, dates, the distinction of weekday and weekend – had no place there.

For the first few weeks they lived a life of quiet formality, as a patient and a hired nurse might live. He ensured that Bella was comfortable, properly medicated and well fed, but they did not talk to each other about themselves. Nothing of their lives, thoughts or past was spoken. This was easy enough since she was still unable to speak. They allowed the difficulty of her having to write everything down to keep their distance from each other. If she chanced to catch him looking at her with something like longing in his eyes, she hurriedly shifted her gaze, giving him time to readjust. Anything personal, like the stilted one-way conversation over the mirror, was necessary, or accidental, but always rapidly covered with practical matters of activity. His devotion to her was as mute as she was obliged to be, and she was grateful not to have to consider why he had turned his life upside down so that he could take care of her.

But it couldn't last forever like that. Three months after he had moved her into the white, immaculately ready house, and when the worst of the pain had finally let up, she answered his 'Good morning' with the first of her own, and as wide a smile as she could manage. He looked astonished and stopped dead, her cup of steaming tea in his hand. It frightened her a little, because she had forgotten that he had never heard her speak until that moment. It crossed her mind, as she watched him slowly react to the new circumstance, that she might suffer the same fate as those silent actresses who had tried to make the move to talking pictures, and rendered themselves ridiculous with their unexpected accents and timbres. Her voice was not absurdly high, nor did it have any noticeable or surprising accent, but it was a *voice* where there had been none, and therefore something of a shock. In fact, it was, if anything, rather husky from want of use, and slightly sibilant because she was still not confident about opening her mouth very far. But it was not, she thought, actually unpleasant.

He seemed to get used to her speaking soon enough, but for a day or two he was almost shy, as if with a voice she was a new person whom he had to get to know. Or perhaps, it was that he felt that she was a new person who had to get to know and accept – or reject – him.

It was a few evenings after that first vocalized 'Good morning' that he came back and knocked on the door of her room.

'I've got a present for you,' he told her shyly, and handed her a brightly coloured, gift-wrapped parcel he had been holding behind his back.

'Oh,' she said, genuinely surprised.

He looked sharply at her, taken aback momentarily by the sound of her voice. It was still new to him to have her speak. When he was away all day, imagining her waiting for him at home, he still imagined her silent.

Bella sat on a chair and began to undo the package, but he looked distressed suddenly, as if he had just thought of something awful, 'Don't take it the wrong way . . .' She had the feeling he might take the package away.

'I like presents,' she said possessively, and continued to unwrap it on her knees. She pulled off the coloured twine, then the shiny red, outer paper, and finally pulled away the layers of white tissue, while his face went through a sequence of uncertainty, anxiety, and finally, outright alarm with each stage of the unwrapping. She looked down at the object which lay revealed surrounded in its swathes of tissue.

It was a mask. It was made of papier mâché and had the face of a sad but beautiful clown. It was the kind of thing which can be seen everywhere, as dolls, or brooches, or sideboard ornaments; and usually they are saccharine and sentimental. But this mask, though it belonged to the same family, was different. It was hand-made, painted carefully and beautifully in chalky white and glossy black, and looked sorrowful and solemn without seeming at all maudlin. And it was not actually a beautiful face, but curiously striking, with a strange, defeated look. It was the cliché of the sad clown brought back to what must once have been its original power to wring the heart. There were almond-shaped holes for the eyes, and at each side were two slits, at temple and jaw level, threaded with ivory satin ribbon the ends of which lay coiled on the wrapping paper.

She stared at the mask, lying in white tissue on her lap, for a moment that must have seemed to him unendurably long. It was a beautiful object, but seeing it so suddenly exposed took her breath away. It was like a forbidden word shouted in a silent room, making one's ears ring with the shock of it.

'Look, I didn't mean it to seem as if I don't like . . . don't want . . . I mean it's nothing to do with your . . .' his words ran out.

Apart from that early conversation about the mirror, neither of them had ever referred to her looks. She thought now that she had

163

come to believe she was invisible, at least to him, and there was no one else to see her. Having no mirror – or not using the mirror they had – allowed her to forget, or, perhaps, misplace the information she had about the way she looked. It stunned her when she realized that for three months since the bandages came off, he had been seeing her, daily, as she really was. It sounded absurd, since her whole life had been transfigured on the day of the accident, to say she could have forgotten her condition, and it was not exactly true, because the moment never passed when she was not aware of it. Yet, in some mind-somersaulting way, because of the quietness of their life in that house, and because of their mutual silence on the subject, the reality of what he saw when he looked at her escaped her. Now, they were both jolted by the truth which lay staring up at her.

'It's just that I was passing this shop where they make things for the theatre, and it was in the window,' he told her in a voice dull with misery.

The silence – her silence – had become unendurable.

'It's astonishing,' she said, without looking up, her voice expressionless.

'I thought we could hang it somewhere. Put it on a wall.'

She couldn't stop herself.

'So there'd be something decent to look at round here?' she snapped, finding rage boiling in her, hissing through her still half-closed lips.

But even before she'd finished speaking, she shook her head to negate the words, to clear the rage away.

'Wait,' she said, taking the mask from its tissue bed, and disappearing upstairs. She left him standing disconsolately with the discarded wrapping paper at his feet, and went up to the bathroom.

She put the mask up to her face, holding it there gingerly, at first, to see if it caused her pain, and then she tied the ribbons behind her head to secure it. She combed her hair forward with her fingers to hang so that it concealed the sides of the mask.

The mask felt strange on her face, suffocating at first, with a paper and glue smell of old classroom in her nostrils. She put her hands up to it and felt it with her fingertips, like a blind person investigating the features of a new acquaintance; the hard contours of cheekbone, sharp nose and wide brow, as if the flesh had petrified and formed a horny shell. Indeed, she thought tartly, she had felt something like this before, when she was in the hospital.

She stood still for a moment, her heart pounding at what she suspected she might be about to do, but she remembered he was in trepidation downstairs. She had no desire to prolong his anxiety about her reaction, so she reached up to the top of the cabinet and turned the key, once she had it in her hand, in the lock. Again, in spite of her concern for him, she stopped for a moment with her hand on the cabinet door. She told herself it was all right; that the mask would prevent her seeing anything she was not ready for. It was a safe first stage, and there need not be a second. She opened the door.

The mirror was propped vertically against the back of the cabinet, its reflecting face turned away, as if he had guessed she might find the key and had taken this precaution against sudden shock. It was about eight inches square, and framed in chrome, with a metal device on the back to allow it to stand freely, or, by reversing the stand, to be hung on a wall. In her procrastination, she had even read the maker's name on the back, although later, try though she might, she couldn't recall it. Finally, she took it in her hand, and shutting her eyes, turned it the right way round, and stood it to face her on the cabinet shelf.

She allowed herself the brief reprieve of a count to ten before she opened her eyes and then saw, staring back at her, as she cheated herself on *nine*, the tragi-comic image of sadness dressed up for the fair. It should not have surprised her; the mask had not changed its nature since she looked at it on the dining table. But there was something new and jarring about it, nevertheless.

It was, of course, nothing to do with the mask, but was caused by the terrified, even terrorized look which lived in the eyes behind the mask. Her own eyes, which she had not seen since

165

she'd glanced at herself in the shop window the moment before the explosion.

She leaned forward. There were the same dark grey irises which almost matched the black pupils, as if they had been shaded by a lead pencil pressed only a little more lightly outside the pupil's circumference. But now, as she continued to peer in at herself, the look in those eyes was no longer of fear, but of curiosity. Her own fright at what she had been about to see had scared her into thinking fear was their habitual expression. She was relieved to find this was not the case. The eyeholes of the mask were only large enough for her to see the pupil, iris and the surrounding white. She could not see the upper or lower lids, so she received no shocking image of damaged or distorted flesh. On the contrary, once the fear had gone from them, she saw what she remembered.

She sighed her relief, and even a little pleasure, and moved back from the mirror to get a larger view. Though her thick, straight hair, falling around the mask, gave it a somewhat more feminine appearance than the usual androgynous quality such masks have when topped by a black skull cap, a foolish, neither-boy-nor-girl creature gazed back at her from the mirror, locked into a sadness which could only come, such was the subtlety of the mask's maker, from a great misunderstanding of the nature of things. A tripping up, as is the clown's stock in trade, of herself on an obstacle that never was there. It was possible to be amused and saddened all at once at the creature in the mirror's bewildered incomprehension of her lot.

'Clown,' she whispered, with a concealed smile, into the mirror, before turning it around as she had found it. She was not at all tempted to look behind the mask. She had done what she could do. She had seen enough of herself for the time being, so she locked the cabinet door on her reflection and put the key back in its not very elusive hiding place.

She called out to him where he still waited in her room.

'I'm going down to the living room. Bring some candles and a bottle of wine.'

He had been sitting glumly on the edge of the bed, staring down at the empty layers of wrapping paper, sick at himself for not having seen what his gift might suggest – what it couldn't fail to suggest. And he expected punishment. He was frightened of what she could do to him. Although he was physically capable of crushing the life out of her with very little effort, he knew that his was always the greater danger between them, because he loved her. Women made you weak. He remembered when she was still unconscious in the hospital and he watched over her, not sure if she was going to live. Even though he didn't know her then, it felt like *his* life was going to end, as if her not being in the world, not being with him, put an end to everything. It was like standing on the edge of the world and knowing that someone was going to push you off into the blackness, and there not being a thing you could do about it. Helplessness. Sometimes, watching her before she came round, he had hated her for the fear she filled him with. But still his heart quaked at the prospect of not having her, of losing her.

He felt as if there was something the matter with him; like he had a disease. A wrongness. Perhaps something went wrong in the making of him. A soft spot. That's what they say: 'I've got a soft spot for you.' They didn't know how right they were when they said that. Being with her – the way he was with her – felt like he was a character in a film, sometimes. No, he corrected himself, more like an advert. One of those rubbishy things for chocolate or scent, where the man risks his neck to give some bint he hardly knows a bunch of flowers or a box of Black Magic. You just laugh at those things. You know it's not meant to be real life. Yet, that was just the way it had been with her. She made a pain in him, just the thought of her. Twisted him up inside. Confusing him. Making him do things he'd be ashamed for anyone to know about – *devoted* things that men aren't supposed to do, not men he knew, anyway. He lost his respect for himself, but he couldn't stop, couldn't help any of it. There she was, in the soft spot in his mind, making him quiver with fear at the thought of not having her around any more for him to love her.

167

She made him frightened to die.

He didn't think she loved him. Not in the way he loved her. Nothing like. Not that love was a pretty thing to him. He was, after all, glad she had been in the café when the bomb exploded; pleased that she was lonely enough not to have anyone close to turn to; grateful for the dreadful facial injuries which kept her dependent on him. It wasn't that his love was vicious, it was simply terrible and pragmatic.

When he had collected the candles and wine, he entered the living room tentatively, and saw her wearing the deadpan black and white clown mask, sitting on the floor in the dark. She held out her hand for a glass which he gave her at arm's length, and then went and sat with the bottle and his glass in the armchair opposite. He said nothing for a long time, but looked unblinking at her, his breathing coming hard. Finally he spoke, his voice harsh and angry with suspicion.

'What are you doing?'

'I think I'm going to need a straw,' she said.

'What?'

Her voice was muffled by the mask.

'A straw,' she repeated, but louder this time. 'You'll have to get some. I'll manage in the mean time.'

She tilted the bottom of the mask up and took a long draught.

'Light the candles.'

'What's going on?' he asked.

He was still waiting for some blow from her in retribution for his gaffe at bringing her the mask, and was consumed with fear that he would lose her now because of what he'd done. He was wrong, she had taken his gift in quite another way, but even if she hadn't, where could she have gone?

'It's all right,' she said.

He lit the room with a dozen white candles, dropping softened wax from their burning tips on to window-sills and the mantel-piece, fixing them upright as the wax hardened. The room glowed with yellow light and shadows that danced on the walls as if a great fire was being reflected. She watched through the eye-holes of her mask as he put the final one in place. Still uncertain, he waited, holding his breath.

'Tell me a story,' she said to him.

'I don't know any stories,' he muttered, sullen and suspicious.

'Tell me about when you found me.' He hesitated. 'Tell me,' she insisted.

He began slowly, carefully, still afraid of what might be going on. But as he spoke, the memory gripped him.

He hadn't known what he was in for, that day when he came on the bomb debris. He hadn't been looking for a change in his life. He wasn't even going to stop. He saw the smoking wreckage from a distance, and thought to himself: Keep out of it. Keep going. It wasn't any of his business.

But he stopped. Maybe out of curiosity more than anything. He made his way through the wreckage even though he didn't reckon anyone would be alive. He wasn't squeamish, but it was a really nasty mess. Everyone he looked at – those who had more or less complete bodies to look at – was well dead. But he saw her arm move, or thought he did. It must have been then it happened to him.

He had knelt down on the floor beside her to see if she was breathing, so that their faces were only inches apart. It was like it was too close, too private, being so near to the face of someone he didn't know from Adam, in such a state. He felt he was looking into someone's bedroom window, watching her undress, and although he realized she needed help urgently, he was paralysed, unable to stop himself from sneaking that secret view. He had no idea how long he stared at her in reality, but it seemed like an age to him. Her head was askew, and her face in a horrible state. It was so bad, he only knew it was a face from its relation to her neck and shoulders. The plate-glass window of the café had smashed under the impact of the blast, throwing her and shards of glass across the room. Blood covered her entire head and bits of shattered glass were sticking into her flesh. He remembered seeing her blink, but he couldn't see her eyes, it was only the movement he noticed. As if someone had thrown a bucket of offal over her; there was just blood and torn flesh where her features should have been. All he could make out was the rough outline. But as he stared, at first, maybe, to prove to himself he was as hard as he thought he was, he began to see underneath the mess.

He tried to retrieve the vision he'd had as he sat opposite her in the candle-lit room, but it was almost impossible. It was as if he'd seen through the blood and gore to her *real* face. He knew it was impossible, but it was the only way he could remember it. He saw her as she really was, her face untouched, more than untouched – and that was when he fell in love with her.

Later, trying to understand it, he began to think that there was some kind of pattern in everyone's head, a sort of picture of an ideal face which each person had. Maybe, it was someone they'd known when they were a kid, or just someone they'd seen, or their mother or something, but it was there, and all the time, as you go about, you look at the faces that pass by or you meet, and try and match them up to the one in your mind. He didn't mean people *knew* they were doing it – he didn't quite know what he meant – but he thought that was what happened anyway. So, very occasionally, you come across a match – it would have to be a perfect match – and then, that was it, you'd had it, you were hooked. It wouldn't matter what they were like, or what they did, they'd got you, and you'd have to get them, it wouldn't matter what it cost. Anyway, that's what he'd thought about it. He couldn't figure it any other way. Once he saw her real face through the blood and glass, even though he didn't know how he could have, it was done. It was something that had happened to him, and he couldn't do a thing about it. It wasn't that the face he saw was particularly beautiful. It wasn't a face like models had, or even the kind of face he specially went for under normal circumstances when he was out of a weekend and looking for a bit of fun. She wasn't even all that young. It was just *his* face; the face he'd got stuck in his mind. Stuck with, that was it exactly. He was a sheet of flypaper and her face was a fly that got stuck on it. A sort of accident, like the one he saw as he passed on his motorbike. One that changed your life.

What he remembered about the face he had seen was that it was almost round in shape, with arched, semi-circular eyebrows, very strong and dark, above eyes of a dark, incredible grey. The way they looked at him, those eyes, even though they *weren't* really looking at him or anything else, and anyway were almost completely veiled in blood, was like she knew he wouldn't be able to walk away from her, that having seen her, she knew he was hooked. It was crazy, he knew, because that was hardly what could have been on her mind, but that was what he saw in the perfect face underneath the mess it had become. Her mouth was quite wide, and slightly open, but the lips were soft and relaxed, not tense in that way you see when women think they're being sized up. Anyway, it was *that* face: that was the point, and as he looked at it, like he was looking at a picture, his heart started thumping in the way it does if you have a narrow squeak, a sort of mixture of delayed terror and the thrill that you're not dead after all. And there it was.

If he'd been a painter, he could have painted the face, and it would have made sense. It was the shape, more than anything, and the way the features were arranged . . . or their size in that particular shape . . . he didn't know. He'd thought about the Mona Lisa and other paintings he'd seen illustrated of women, not nudes, just faces – portraits. He reckoned those painters had the same thing he did in their minds, but they could paint the faces they had in their heads. Maybe, there didn't have to be a real woman, or they might have rearranged some ordinary woman's features on the canvas so it was more like their ideal. If he could draw, he'd have sketched the face in his head, until his fingers bled, just so he could look at it without the bother of having to find the actual woman. He didn't suppose it would have helped. He didn't think anything helped. You'd still find yourself staring into that face on a real woman one day, and that would be that. It wouldn't matter what kind she was: a real slag or a fucking princess, if she had that face, you'd be lost.

He didn't know if it was like that for women. He didn't think it could be, but maybe that was just because he'd never been *the* face

171

in some woman's mind. But women were different. Fuck only knew about women.

He had dipped his face on to hers and given her the kiss of life when he saw her stop breathing in front of his eyes. By the time the paramedics reached her, he came up, dripping with her blood, scored with the jagged bits of glass, and she was alive again. He'd followed her to the hospital. He didn't know why at the time, except he couldn't stop himself from seeing in his mind her face behind the mess. Even then, once she'd gone through the doors in the stretcher, he might have come over sensible, turned around and fucked off, but the Old Bill stopped him. They wanted a statement from him, but *then* he could have gone. Done his good deed for the decade and ridden away. But he didn't. He waited outside the emergency room until the doctor came out and told him there was a chance she'd live.

That was what he'd had to find out. If the doctor had said she was a goner, no chance, he would have turned on his heels, gone back home, had his dinner, said goodnight to the kids, and never thought about her again. Except, there'd have been a picture in his head of that face, but that was always there (though not attached to a person), and most of the time it was something he ignored. As much as he loved her, he sometimes thought it would have been better if she'd died. Better for him, and she'd been in no state to mind whether she lived or not. They said he'd saved her life with his kiss. He didn't wish she *was* dead, but maybe he wished she had died.

When he heard she was going to live, he turned round, but not to go home to his life. He bought a local paper and found himself a room. At first, the landlady thought he was a bit rough for her genteel boarding-house. She gave him a proper look in his leathers, his helmet hanging from his wrist, and his machine, black and hot outside her neat front gate. But he had always been a bit of a talker when it suited him. He told her about his sister in the hospital, and looked at her in that way that always works with middle-aged women, and before he knew it he was in the front room with a nice cup of tea in his hand. In a way, what he told her was true, and what was even more true was the state she saw he was in. He didn't have to act upset (although he thought he was acting at the time), for her to start to feel motherly towards him. Funny that, thinking you're conning someone, but really being sincere without knowing it.

It was weeks before she was anything you could call conscious. It didn't make much sense sitting there night after night. She didn't know if he was there or not. But he had to do it. It was like he had devoted his life to her, in a religious sort of way. Not that he'd thought about it then, but if he ever decided to be a priest he figured it would feel like his decision to take care of her. It wasn't so different from finding a vocation, really: he gave up everything in an instant, including, it seemed, sex. He just walked away from his life without a thought for what he was doing. All he knew was that it had to be like that. He had no choice. If he'd suddenly been struck with a belief in God, it would have been the same. And she, in those early days, was about as real as God. She was still and silent, wrapped in bandages. She was invisible, you couldn't see anything of her – it was an act of faith believing there was anyone there at all. But he knew.

And that was it. He never went home. He called Mary and told her he wasn't coming back. She had a good scream at him down the phone. He didn't think it was that she cared much about him – he was never a model husband, she'd had it with him staying out nights and not helping much with the kids – but she was *married*, which is what she wanted to be. He told her he'd make sure she had money for the house and kids, and herself, and that he'd pick up some clothes from the house the next day when she was at work. She said he'd better get there fucking early because his things would be out on the street (which they were, suitcases and loose shoes spread over the pavement, when he went round the next day), and he'd better not try to see the kids again. He felt numb about it all. He didn't dislike Mary, he was genuinely fond of her, and he loved the kids. He felt as married as Mary did. He'd screwed around, and spent most of his spare time with the lads, but that didn't mean he didn't want the old woman at home

173

waiting for him when he got there. It was a marriage like most marriages; nothing romantic about it, but they were used to each other. She didn't have much to complain about – he always made sure she had plenty of housekeeping and nice clothes for her and the kids, she worked because she wanted to, and when they had sex, it wasn't bad. And he didn't thump her or anything.

They'd married because she fell for a kid, and neither of them pretended it was a big romantic deal. He hadn't wanted that. But he didn't mind having kids and being married – he was ready for it, and Mary and him got on well enough. They went to the pub together and although they never talked about it – or anything much – she knew he'd been screwed up by a woman before he met her. Suzy had been another version of *that* face, the only other one. He'd loved her, but she'd lost interest pretty quickly, his not being *that* face for her. Mary just sort of let him lean on her. Early on, when they were going together, after they'd fucked, sometimes he would cry. He couldn't help himself. The business with Suzy wasn't out of his system. The shame of it was terrible, but Mary didn't laugh or ask questions. She'd hold him quietly, and kind of rock him until he fell asleep, and the next morning she wouldn't mention it. He was grateful to her for that.

But once they were married, and Suzy had eventually sunk back into the past of his life, he'd started playing around with other women. He felt settled with Mary, but he needed other women for sex, or rather, he needed sex, and not the kind he and Mary had.

He wanted women he didn't know, and whom he wouldn't know when they'd finished. He liked it best if he didn't even know their names, though mostly you had to buy them a drink and have a bit of a conversation first. He wasn't looking for someone special, so it had nothing to do with Mary, in a way. He wanted to fuck. To fuck, to fuck and to fuck. He felt like he deserved it, that fucking women fucking owed it to him. They were tits and cunts and mouths he used for coming. He didn't want to hurt them, particularly, but he didn't want to know them, or anything about them. He just wanted them lying there under him with their fucking clothes off and him sticking it in them, everywhere and anywhere it would fit. Then he didn't want to see them again. Mostly, he preferred to do it in his car, or even in the street, in dark alleyways. He couldn't take them home, of course, and he wouldn't go to their places. He didn't want to know where they lived, or see their night-dresses and bedrooms, any more than he wanted to know their names.

Then he'd go home and Mary would be in bed, sulking. It didn't bother him much; he didn't take any notice. At weekends, if he had no job on, he'd spend a bit of time with the kids. He'd take them to the park or something. It seemed to him a pretty normal way to live, and he thought even now that it was the same for Mary, too. He was never going to get romantically involved again, he was certain of that, and he'd got himself settled well enough, he figured, into a routine that was no different from the lives of most of his mates.

And then, from one minute to the next, he was off with some woman he didn't even know. Never mind didn't know, had never really seen. It was the melodrama of it that burned Mary up. He thought he could understand that. There they were, settled, going on in the usual way. It wasn't wonderful, not for him or her, but it was like they'd both agreed that what they had was normal and good enough for them. They weren't film stars. And then, suddenly, he changed the rules. If he looked at it from her point of view, he supposed she must have felt cheated; left with two kids and off he'd gone into the sunset. She was right, he'd welshed on their deal. But he'd really believed he had finished with the love stuff, and that all he wanted was the usual: an ordinary family and a bit of dirty sex on the side. She was right to feel cheated. He was pretty sure she'd find another bloke – she was good looking and a born wife – and have a couple more kids by him, but she'd been cheated out of the romance she must have had in her head when she was young. Mary had settled for marriage with him at eighteen, before she'd had a big romance, and her chances now of taking one look at someone, sparks flying and going off with them were pretty small, what with the kids and the house, and ageing.

To tell the truth, he thought she was better off without it. He wondered what she'd think if she knew he'd left her for a woman a good few years older than himself and with no face?

Well, it didn't matter now, but as far as he was concerned, she had a face all right. She had *the* face, behind the blood and glass, behind the bandages, behind the disguise of her shiny, distorted, rigid, grafted skin, behind the mask; it was there always, as beautiful to him as beautiful could be. And always those eyes looked out, like they'd stared at him, into him, that first moment when he knelt down and peered at her. The deep, weird grey, like eyes shouldn't be, which pulled him in until, sometimes, it was as if he'd been sucked behind them and saw out of them himself. Her face was what he wanted more than anything. More than family, more than sex.

He used to take her flowers. That was when he had to admit that something out of order was going on. Before that, everything he did was like in a dream. He didn't *think* about renting a place near the hospital, or phoning Mary, or going back to the room the next night after he had done the job: he just *did* those things. But when he suddenly saw himself in a darkened window, standing at the nurses' desk with a big bunch of flowers he'd just paid good money for from the stall downstairs, he realized something very odd was happening. He'd never given flowers to a woman in his life, not since he was a kid and bought a bunch for his mum on Mother's Day, and then that rose he'd given Suzy, being the idiot he'd been for a while. He wasn't like that, not really. He thought of himself as straightforward. If he wanted a woman, he let her know it, and she would say yes or no. Of course, there were the ones who wanted more than a 'Want a fuck, yes or no?', and he didn't mind buying a couple of drinks and chatting them up a bit, but even then he made sure they knew what he wanted before he went up to the bar. No candlelight or flowers. You fancy someone; you want to fuck them. Simple. And there weren't many women who complained. At least no one could say he led them up the garden path. No flowers; no garden path. Right?

So, standing there holding a bunch of bloomers he'd paid

fifteen quid for, with the nurse staring down at them practically with tears in her eyes with pity for him, he felt like a complete prat. *Then*, he should have buggered off. When he knew how bad things were. But, the fact was, things were so bad that he didn't go. He ignored the pity and went into the side room to sit with the bandage-masked woman whose name he had yet to discover. And when the nurse came in with a vase and offered to put the flowers in water for him and how nice they were, he just said, 'Thank you'. He was a goner, and he knew it.

It turned out she didn't like brightly coloured flowers, anyway. She liked things white. But he didn't know that then, and it didn't matter because she never saw them for weeks. They stood in a tall vase on the locker beside her bed, as she lay flat on her back with her eyes closed to everyone but him. Every two days he brought new ones in, and the nurse threw away the last lot and arranged them. Once he'd started, there was no way to stop. The flowers, he meant, but everything else, too, now he came to think of it.

Him, with bunches of flowers in his hand, and when she said she wanted white ones, white fucking bunches of flowers in his hand. Him. Yes, him. That's how it was. He shouldn't have been surprised at himself because it had happened before, but he had been so sure he'd never let it happen again: and with Suzy it was different. She'd hit him hard, but he was younger, and he hadn't changed his whole life for her. Not quite. He wasn't married then, no kids; he didn't turn anyone else's world upside down. But the truth was, he would have. It would have been the same thing; he'd have walked away from anything and everything if she'd given him the chance. There was one thing about falling in love with an unconscious woman; she couldn't stop you wrecking your life. She couldn't tell you to fuck off, or disappear on you. You've got your ruination just where you want her, and there's not a sodding thing she can do about it. That was power for you.

'I loved you from the moment I first saw you,' he said.

She pressed a forefinger to her false black mouth and reached over to plant it on his lips.

'Put out the candles,' she told him. 'I'm going to bed, now.'

Bella had no intention of sleeping. She lay awake on top of her bed with the mask still on until there was that special silence of the early hours of the morning. When everything had been still for a long time, she got up and, in her clown mask and night-dress, went down to the floor below, where he slept. She opened his door and for the first time entered his room. A nearby street light shone on his naked torso. Large as he was, he looked vulnerable in his sleep. He lay on his back with one arm flung out over the side of the bed, his palm up and open as if it were waiting to receive something.

She pulled the cover right away from him, and, lifting the skirt of her night-dress, climbed carefully on top of his naked, sleeping body. He didn't wake as she settled herself astride him and slowly lowered herself until the inside of her thighs met the flesh of his belly.

He opened his eyes, then, and jerked in alarm at seeing the sad clown hovering over him.

'What?' he gasped.

She put a finger to her papier-mâché lips to quieten him, and carefully, so as not to dislodge the mask, lifted the night-dress slowly over her shoulders and head, letting it fall behind her on the bed. He lay quite still now, staring at her. A long moment passed.

'Take it off,' he said, hoarsely.

She was naked apart from the mask. She shook her head.

'Take it off,' he said again, and reached up behind her head to untie the ribbons.

She took his hands away, shaking her head again, and placed them on her breasts, then ran a finger around the contour of his mouth. When she had completed the movement, she slipped the finger between his lips, which parted and drew in breath as her finger caressed the inside of his cheeks, and played down along the length of his tongue. His mouth tightened around it, and he sucked hard and rhythmically on her finger, making deep sounds in his throat. A sudden spasm of desire, sharp enough to sever an artery, rose up in her, ripping through her lower body, hardening her breasts, making her head sing with the rushing sound of the sea.

She pressed one of his hands hard against her breast and remained motionless, not breathing, only feeling the astonishing wave whip around inside her like a terrible, trapped beast. It broke free, finally, in a cry which issued from behind the mask through her open mouth, throwing her head back and shaking her body as if she were having a seizure.

'More . . . more . . . more . . .' she panted, still in the grip of the climax which had begun with nothing more than the pressure of his mouth on her forefinger, his hand against her breast, but now demanded more. He lifted her hips and placed his penis at the entrance of her vagina, and then, passive again, let her lower herself on to him. She moved up and down on him slowly, again and again, pressing down harder with each thrust, widening the angle of her thighs, and manoeuvring until he was so deeply inside her she thought her heart and lungs would implode from the pressure.

Did she love him? Not then. Then, she was caught up in a private, personal passion that used his body as a machine to release her banked-up energy, as if it were a scalpel to free the pus from a boil. She was in a rage of sexual agitation, and somewhere in the centre of her was an image of damaged, broken bodies and lives shattering like glass and throwing their shards around the container that was her. He didn't even exist at that moment; there was only her howling in her own ears.

She could not stop. She could not finish. Climax merged into climax without ever achieving a final release. It was a madness of possession which refused to let her go. Eventually, he pulled her down against his chest and held her tightly, tightly, in his arms, bringing her down from her terrible height, like a father putting his weeping child to sleep, soothing and whispering the words adults say to frightened children. He took no pleasure of his own, except perhaps in his holding of her. They had never touched more than hands before.

Gradually, she quietened, and they were left with just the

179

rhythm of their two hearts beating, one on top of the other. It was only then that she noticed him. His gentleness and apparent understanding of what was going on in her was astonishing to her. There were whores, she had heard, who would do anything with a man, except kiss him. It made complete sense to her. Lying breast against breast on him, with his arm protectively around, was like that – an unacceptable intimacy after the hungry sex. She raised herself up and put her robe back on. He stayed still and watchful, as she climbed off him and stood, clothed and still masked, beside his bed.

She took his silence to be uncertainty. She wanted to make it clear that nothing had changed.

'That won't happen again,' she said.

For a moment he looked the way actors make cowboys look in westerns when they're shot. That expression of dull surprise on a face that is half-way towards death. She used to think it was no more than an actorly convention, but his face took on exactly the same look. And she, like a moral sheriff, took no pleasure in pulling the trigger, she only did what she had to do.

Then his face changed, absorbing the pain.

'Sometimes,' he said.

She shook her head.

'Sometimes,' he repeated. It wasn't a question.

'Sometimes,' she conceded, not really agreeing, but putting the conversation aside. 'But it can't change the way things are.'

'Right then,' he said, his voice sour with sarcasm. 'We'll have a mask evening once a month, like periods.'

'I've never had them,' she told him as she opened the door. 'I never bleed.'

He loves me, she told herself. He wouldn't just leave. How would she manage? He loves me, she thought again fiercely. There was no doubt of that. He can't help but come back. Soon, he'd be back. How could she be left so utterly alone? It would be all right.

But she knew it wouldn't.

6

———

At the bedside Sister Fredericks and the doctor considered their patient.

'Bella's improved a lot since she was brought in,' Sister Fredericks said.

'She might make it. I think she's going to be all right,' the doctor replied. 'And Mrs Georgiou? How's she coming along?'

The voices she heard were so close they could only be refering to her. Brought in? From where? To where? She lay with her eyes closed, unable to form any picture of either of these places: the where she had been or the where she was now. Another blankness formed as she tried to imagine the who who had 'brought her in' or the who who stood over her now and thought she was going to be all right. Even being all right was a concept that triggered no simple explanation in her mind. So Bella is going to be all right. Well, good. But who is Bella?

Gradually, the condition of the woman in Bed 7 improved. She began to take nourishment and a bombardment of antibiotics worked their regular miracle of fighting infection. She started to look human again, even to sit up. Once she had fully come round, Sister Fredericks sat on the edge of her bed.

'Feeling a little better, now?' she asked. 'Want to talk? What's your name?'

The woman looked hard at Sister Fredericks, seeming to be searching for something in her face.

'I don't know,' she said, with a look of alarm.

'Do you remember anything? Where you came from? Why you were living on the streets?'

The woman looked baffled.

'Was I?' She thought again. 'I don't remember anything at all.'

It was an ordinary voice, London bred, gruff from illness and alcohol. Sister Fredericks smiled.

'Never mind. It'll come back. But we'd better give you a name, just for the time being. Is there any name you'd like us to call you?' Sister Fredericks wasn't happy with the name the paramedics had given the tramp when she was brought in. Now that she was awake and talking, there was something cruel about it. She walked to the end of the bed and crossed it off the chart.

The woman shook her head, more surprised than distressed at the emptiness inside her head.

'What's your name?' she asked the sister.

'Annie. Annie Fredericks.'

'That'll do. Call me Annie.'

'Well, I take that as a compliment,' Sister Fredericks smiled, getting up and writing Annie on the chart on the end of the bed. 'OK, Annie, how do you fancy a little something to eat?'

7

Mimi woke from the first dream she had ever recollected. She laughed out loud as she remembered it.

Picture the colour green, not as it might immediately spring to mind – the green of summer trees, of grass – but something paler, though in no way insipid, and mixed with a tinge of blue. Turquoise, perhaps, but not the first bright turquoise that you would imagine – not the vibrancy of eastern silks or the semi-precious stone – though it *is* vivid. A flatter sea green, but startling and strange, or, at any rate, of a tone which causes a strangeness in the chest and tightens the throat. *That* kind of strange. *That* kind of green. Do you see it?

It is the sea, though not quite the colour of any sea you've seen before. Which is why when it appears so suddenly, as it does, you gasp. The colour alone would be enough to take your breath away, but the magnitude of this sea is heart-stopping. It bursts upon you without warning, this sea-green expanse, entirely filling your field of vision, and it's a boisterous sea, not still and glacial, but rugged and choppy. It's almost wild, almost dangerous. The strength of it, the size, and the colour affront you, as if your eyes have been shut for aeons, accustomed only to blankness, then opened shockingly to this vivid immensity. Which is precisely how it is, or seems; you might not have existed before this moment.

Once you've caught your breath, released the gasp and taken in calmer air, you realize that you are on a boat, a small ferry, standing up at the front, in the open with nothing but a railing between you and the sea beneath, in front, and all around. The boat leaps like a dolphin in the lively waves, and the sea-green, not-quite-turquoise spray hits your face.

You have come out of some quiet harbour into the open sea, you understand, but the first thing you knew was the sight of this extraordinary body of water on which you ride, with no land in sight ahead or to either side of you (you do not look behind you, you do not think of doing that).

Only, now, there is something ahead. A speck at first, but it grows rapidly. The boat is rollicking in the waves and you find you are approaching a tower planted in the middle of the sea like a tiny island. There is no land around it, just the tower rising out of the water, tall, several stories high, and made of red brick, not beautiful, nor circular, but four-square and solid; something the industrial Victorians might have made, a building with a purpose. It makes you think of railway architecture, or electricity sub-stations, except that it is forty foot tall and stranded in the middle of this vast sea-green sea.

You come nearer to it, still feeling the cold wash on your face, and the salt taste on your lips – you are settled enough now into your surroundings to run your tongue absent-mindedly around your mouth. Now you see the detail, you are close enough, the ferry even seems to be slowing down. There is a metal staircase running up the outside of the tower, nothing fancy, plain, like a fire escape. It ends at the top at a door, the only door you can see on the face of the tower as you approach it. There are windows at the top, too, to either side of the door, but nothing below, no windows or doors, only blind brick.

The ferry has stopped. You have already disembarked. Even now you are climbing the stairs of the tower in a file of fellow passengers. You are in the middle. People ahead of you are disappearing through the door at the top, and you know, though you don't look back, that there are people following behind you. There seems to be no hurry, nor any alarm. Nothing surprising is happening, it's routine, this journey up to the top of the tower. You know that, though you also know you have not reached your destination; wherever that may be, it is not here.

It dawns on you, as you reach the doorway, that there is a logic to this and once you have had the thought, it comes clear that this tower is a toll-house through which all passengers crossing this sea have to pass. The ferry will be waiting on the other side, you are certain. As everything seems to fall into place, you forget to wonder that there should be a toll-house in the middle of an ocean. It seems perfectly natural to you.

Now you have passed through the door and entered the top room of the tower. In front of you, across the room, is another open door, leading out to the exterior stairway on the other side. The queue of passengers is filing through the doorway which is held open for them by an official in uniform. You remember him from the ferry; he is the captain, you think, but then correct yourself, he is the conductor, that is the right description. It is his job to ensure the passage through the toll-house goes smoothly, so that he and you can all re-join the ferry and continue the journey.

As you approach the opposite door – there are half-a-dozen people in front of you – you look around. It is an empty room with a bare wooden floor, and you can see the water through the windows which are on all four sides. Then you glance behind and to the left and realize the room is not merely an empty shell. By the door through which you entered, there is a windowed alcove, set back from the room (if you'd kept looking straight ahead, like everyone else, in the direction you were going, you'd never have seen it). A bed fits into the alcove, and on it, stretched out full length, on her side, resting one elbow on the pale spread with her head propped on her hand, is a woman. She is wearing loose clothes in smoky grey-green colours, and her reddish hair falls over her face and shoulders and though you cannot see her features, she is concentrated on a large notebook on the bed, in which she is writing. She takes no notice of the procession of strangers through her room, though you are sure she is aware of you all. Her writing absorbs her, and you see her pen filling the page.

When you reach the other door, you speak to the conductor about the woman.

'Doesn't she find it distracting to have all these people passing through her room?' you ask, indicating the woman on the bed.

'No,' he tells you. 'That's the price for being in a room with such a view.'

You can see that. In order to live surrounded by that extraordinary sea in silence and solitude for most of the time, it would be worth putting up with an intermittent parade of strangers who have to pass through the tower in order to continue their journey. Perhaps, after a while, you would stop noticing the intrusion, or be able to stop paying it any attention. You nod your understanding at the conductor and proceed through the door feeling a touch of regret that you, too, are not in such a position as the red-haired woman, for it seems to you to be the perfect existence. But you have to descend the staircase and get back on to the waiting boat which will carry you off on the sea-green sea, still with no land in sight. And you wonder, for the first time, with a curious absence of feeling, if you have a destination at all, and whether the boat ride on the measureless ocean might not itself be all there is . . .